PUFFIN

WHITE FEAR

Tom Palmer is an author and football fan. He is a frequent visitor to schools and libraries to talk about reading, writing and football. He has also worked with the National Literacy Trust, the Reading Agency and the Premier League Reading Stars scheme in his quest to promote a passion for reading among boys.

Tom is the author of the Football Academy and Foul Play series. He lives in Yorkshire with his family where he loves to watch football and run.

Find out more about Tom and read his blog at *www.tompalmer.co.uk*. You can also access a free schools' activity pack about the issues in *White Fear* at Tom's website.

Books by Tom Palmer

The Squad series in reading order:

BLACK OP

WHITE FEAR

Foul Play series in reading order:

FOUL PLAY

DEAD BALL

OFF SIDE

KILLER PASS

OWN GOAL

For younger readers

Football Academy series in reading order:

BOYS UNITED

STRIKING OUT

THE REAL THING

READING THE GAME

FREE KICK

CAPTAIN FANTASTIC

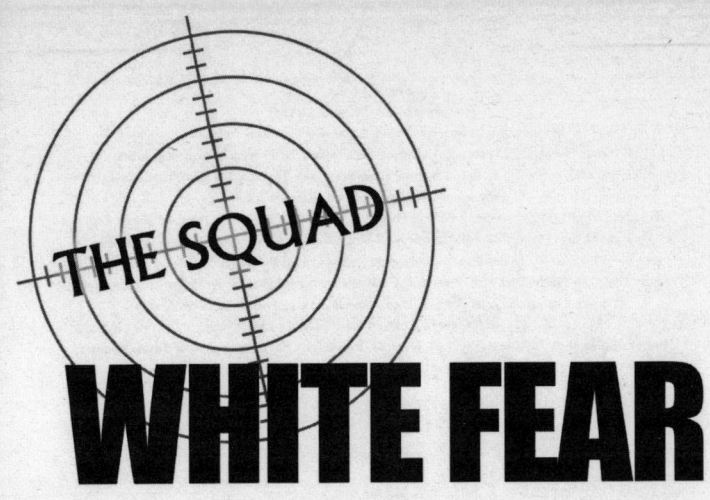

WHITE FEAR

TOM PALMER

To Aimee

Tom Palmer

PUFFIN

PUFFIN BOOKS
Published by the Penguin Group
Penguin Books Ltd, 80 Strand, London WC2R ORL, England
Penguin Group (USA) Inc., 375 Hudson Street, New York, New York 10014, USA
Penguin Group (Canada), 90 Eglinton Avenue East, Suite 700, Toronto, Ontario, Canada M4P 2Y3
(a division of Pearson Penguin Canada Inc.)
Penguin Ireland, 25 St Stephen's Green, Dublin 2, Ireland (a division of Penguin Books Ltd)
Penguin Group (Australia), 250 Camberwell Road, Camberwell, Victoria 3124, Australia
(a division of Pearson Australia Group Pty Ltd)
Penguin Books India Pvt Ltd, 11 Community Centre, Panchsheel Park, New Delhi – 110 017, India
Penguin Group (NZ), 67 Apollo Drive, Rosedale, Auckland 0632, New Zealand
(a division of Pearson New Zealand Ltd)
Penguin Books (South Africa) (Pty) Ltd, Block D, Rosebank Office Park, 181 Jan Smuts Avenue,
Parktown North, Gauteng 2193, South Africa

Penguin Books Ltd, Registered Offices: 80 Strand, London WC2R ORL, England

puffinbooks.com

First published 2012
001

Text copyright © Tom Palmer, 2012
All rights reserved

The moral right of the author has been asserted

Typeset by Palimpsest Book Production Ltd, Falkirk, Stirlingshire
Set in 13/16pt Baskerville MT Std
Printed in Great Britain by Clays Ltd, St Ives plc

Except in the United States of America, this book is sold subject to the condition that it shall not, by way of
trade or otherwise, be lent, re-sold, hired out, or otherwise circulated without the publisher's prior consent in
any form of binding or cover other than that in which it is published and without a similar condition
including this condition being imposed on the subsequent purchaser

British Library Cataloguing in Publication Data
A CIP catalogue record for this book is available from the British Library

ISBN: 978-0-141-33781-4

www.greenpenguin.co.uk

Penguin Books is committed to a sustainable
future for our business, our readers and our planet.
This book is made from Forest Stewardship
Council™ certified paper.

ALWAYS LEARNING　　　　　　**PEARSON**

To Rifleman Jim Sells

MONDAY

FALLING DOWN

Four children crouched motionless on the top of the tallest building in the most northern city in the world, waiting for the order to jump.

Around them were some of the most spectacular views they had ever seen: vast snow-topped crags, deep gorges with fjords running through them, a row of black mountains in the distance. But they weren't there to look at the scenery. The trip was strictly business, not pleasure.

A fifth child – Lesh – sat in a wheelchair, waiting to relay that order and send the other four over the top. For Lesh, this was the first outing since his accident on their last mission. An accident that had left him paralysed from the waist downwards. So today he was determined to get everything right. To the second.

'Remind me why we're doing this?' Adnan, a stocky Asian boy, murmured to the two girls crouching next to him.

One was white with blonde hair. Lily.

The other black with tight dark plaits. Hatty.

'There's someone we need to talk to,' Kester, the fourth member of the group, said. 'And this is the only way of reaching him.'

'Who?' Hatty asked.

'I'm not allowed to say.'

'Thirty seconds,' Lesh said.

'Why not?' Hatty pressed.

'Orders.'

'And why do *you* know and *we* don't?'

'I'm the leader,' Kester said firmly.

'Twenty seconds,' Lesh said, concentrating on his watch.

Lily listened to the others bickering, but decided not to join in. She too was trying to work out what was going on.

The point was that they were not supposed to meet or to be introduced to anybody new. The five of them were a secret. So secret, in fact, that only their commander and their commander's commander knew about them.

Their role?

To travel around the world and carry out black-op missions to save British lives.

Their name?

The Squad.

Five children who work for the British government, spying in the places that ordinary spies cannot reach.

'Ten seconds.'

'Bear in mind it's windy,' Kester warned. 'As you fall, it will affect your descent.'

Lily shifted her feet and prepared to move, her mind still whirring. Who, she asked herself, was this person they were going to meet? Why was he about to find out who they were? And why could they only meet him like this?

'Five.'

The four children stood as one.

'Four.

'Three.

'Two.

'One.'

'Go,' Kester said in a low voice.

And, with that, four children threw themselves over the side of the building.

Lily felt her rope tighten almost as soon as she began to fall. She released it, hand over hand, her three friends moving down at the same pace. Lily felt her feet bounce twice on the side of the building as she descended, then land on something solid.

A balcony.

Without wasting a second – a second in which they might be seen from below – the four children pushed open a pair of large glass doors and entered the warmth of a huge room, lavishly decorated with a large chandelier, oil paintings and a plush red carpet.

'Shut the door,' the woman facing them ordered.

Adnan, the last one in, eased the door to and the four Squad members found themselves facing a man and the woman who had spoken. The woman, with bright copper hair, was no stranger to them. She was Julia, their commander. The man, however, *was* a surprise.

Even though the four Squad members, as trained spies, were supposed to be able to mask their reactions and appear as if nothing could shock them, Lily heard at least two of her friends quietly gasp. Because they all knew exactly who the man was. His face was in the newspapers and on the TV every day. He was about as famous as you could be.

They were looking at the British Prime Minister.

And now they knew that this mission, high in the Arctic Circle, was going to be their most dangerous and most exciting to date.

WORLD WAR THREE

'Good morning... er... children,' the Prime Minister said.

They were standing in an astonishing hotel suite, all of them stunned into silence. It had three sofas, a giant TV screen and a large desk strewn with papers. The walls were decorated with a green and gold leaf pattern. Real gold. Beyond the desk was the massive window that opened out on to the amazing view they had seen from the roof: Norway's northernmost city and its magnificent surroundings.

Hatty was smiling. Smiling because she couldn't believe that the Squad were meeting the British Prime Minister. This was the man who was in control of their country. If they were meeting *him* – and he was telling them what to do *in person* – whatever mission Julia had for them, it was going to be serious. Deadly serious.

Face to face, the Prime Minister looked smaller than he did on the television. He also looked uneasy.

His face was flushed. He was fidgeting with his hands. From the far end of the room he was watched by a young man who was holding a file of documents and wearing a pair of expensive sunglasses.

The Prime Minister cleared his throat. 'We've brought you to the Arctic for a reason,' he said. Then he paused, still seemingly unsure as to how he should talk to them. Hatty knew what this was about: the Prime Minister wasn't used to giving orders to children.

'Please, sir,' Julia said. 'Brief them as you would brief me. The children need to understand the sensitivity of the mission.'

The Prime Minister looked at Julia, hesitated, then tried again.

'This week there's a very important conference taking place here in Norway,' he said. 'Let me explain. All the nations that have a claim to the seabed beneath the Arctic ice . . . the *melting* Arctic ice . . . well, they're here . . . to discuss who owns which part of that seabed.'

Kester understood what the PM meant. 'Norway, Canada, Russia, the United States, Denmark, Iceland.' He reeled off a list of the countries involved. 'They need to work out how to divide the seabed up without a war starting.'

The Prime Minister looked more relaxed. 'To put it simply, yes. If we can convince them to sign a Tromsø Treaty – an agreement as to who owns what in the Arctic – then it will most definitely prevent a war.'

'You're chairing the conference because you're neutral,' Lily added. 'I read about it in a Norwegian newspaper on the flight.'

'A Norwegian newspaper? Do you know Norwegian?'

'Lily knows several languages, sir,' Kester clarified.

'Very good,' the Prime Minister said. 'I'm impressed. You'll know what's really at stake here. The truth is that under the seabed, here in the Arctic, there are billions of pounds' worth of oil and gas and other resources. Trillions in fact. Added to that – and as I'm sure you know – the world is fast running out of oil and gas. Therefore, whichever country can get its hands on that oil and gas will be rich and strong and far more powerful than any other nation. If one country does get the lion's share, it will, effectively, rule the world.'

'Which is why there might be a war,' Hatty said, speaking for the first time. 'Because oil means war.'

The Prime Minister closed his eyes again and nodded. 'Yes. You're absolutely right. The chance of a war is growing by the day. But there doesn't *have* to be a war. If we can stop the people who want to disrupt this conference, then we can – and we will – avoid it.'

'We?' Hatty asked.

The Prime Minister smiled at Hatty. Lily smiled

too: she was always interested to see how adults reacted to Hatty's blunt questions and remarks. But that was Hatty for you.

'*You* are the "we",' the Prime Minster said. 'Look. I'm not happy that we're using . . . I mean . . . working with . . . you . . . with children, but really we have no choice.'

'We're a very experienced unit, sir,' Kester said.

'Yes, so I've heard.' The Prime Minister was looking at the four children as if he was trying to make sense of them. 'But tell me how the *football* element of your cover works. I know about you, but very little about what you do.'

'It started in Poland, sir,' Kester explained.

'Yes?'

'We needed to be able to get into places without being identified as spies. Anywhere in the world. And no one would suspect a kids' football team of espionage.'

'That's true. But what about the other players, your teammates?' the Prime Minister asked. 'Do they know about what you do?'

'No, sir.'

'That must be very tricky. I mean, to hide it from them.'

'We keep the two worlds separate,' Kester said. 'We take precautions. Like any spy ring.'

The Prime Minister nodded. 'Good. As you know, we've organized for you to be involved in a tournament here for just that purpose. USA, Canada, Norway and yourselves. I'm looking forward to seeing you play. I'm a huge soccer fan myself.'

Lily winced. She hated to hear English people call football 'soccer'. It made it seem like they didn't know what they were talking about.

'Sir,' Julia broke in. 'The conference. We need the children to understand the sensitivity of this mission.'

'Indeed,' the Prime Minister said, focusing.

'Can I ask . . . ?' Kester interrupted.

'Yes?'

'Well, can I ask *why* anyone would try to disrupt the conference? I mean, why would they want to spoil the chance of a Tromsø Treaty?'

'Julia?' The Prime Minister passed the question on to the Squad's commander.

'We suspect several people,' Julia explained. 'We have intelligence to indicate that someone may be planning to undo the work the Prime Minister is doing here. That is, to make sure no agreement happens. Perhaps they think that, if there really is a war, then their country would get more oil than if everyone just made a group decision. It's basic greed, really. We need you to find out what these people are planning.'

'Who would want to do that?' Hatty asked.

'We'll go into it later, Hatty,' Julia said quickly. 'Let's not bother the Prime Minister with that now. The fact is someone is planning to undermine the conference. We know that.'

'The *who* is related to the *why*.' The Prime Minister interrupted Julia this time, glancing at his watch. 'But the truthful answer is we don't know which of them it is, so we don't know why exactly they want to do it. But we *do* know that, if the Tromsø Treaty doesn't come off, some of the countries involved are ready to start drilling now in places they shouldn't be.'

'For instance, sir?' Julia pressed.

'For instance? Well, Russia has a fleet of ice-breaking ships and massive oil-drilling ships that they could take to places that maybe aren't Russian, and they may start drilling just to see what happens, to test how another country reacts.'

'So why us?' Hatty asked. 'This is a big deal. Is it something suited to us? Surely this is down to politicians or adult spies. I don't see why you need children to do this for you.'

'That's the point,' the Prime Minister said. 'The only adults allowed in this hotel to attend the conference are government officials. Like Mr Luxton over there.'

The Prime Minister pointed at the silent young man holding the file in the corner.

'There are going to be no maids to service the bedrooms, just to make sure no undercover officer from any country is posing as a hotel worker. Prime ministers are going to have to make their own beds! Therefore, no spies can be here. It's the perfect way to keep things fair. In fact, the only people staying at this hotel, other than known government officials and the UN soldiers making sure that everyone sticks to the agreement, are you and the other three teams taking part in your football tournament. All of you children.'

'And because we're children,' Hatty said, 'no one will suspect us.'

'Exactly,' the Prime Minister said. 'And all the Arctic Powers agree that having innocent children and sport around the conference sends a good message to the world.'

'That we are the future,' Lily said. 'That you're saving the world for the children.'

'It's good to think about the children.' Adnan spoke before the Prime Minister could reply. 'But isn't this terrible for the planet? Surely more oil coming out of the seabed means more global warming. That's no good for the polar bears.'

The Prime Minister put his hand to his mouth and spoke again. 'If we can encourage the countries involved to drill for oil in controlled and cleaner ways, then it's the best we can hope for. More chaotic drilling or a war would make it far worse for the wildlife. Don't you think?'

There was an uneasy silence.

'So, can you help me?' the Prime Minister asked.

All four children said yes as one.

'Good.' The Prime Minister smiled, stepping forward. 'Now, please, do tell me your names.'

None of the children spoke.

Then Kester broke the silence. 'It's probably best, sir, that you don't know our names.'

After the children had shared a tray of soft drinks with the Prime Minister, Julia signalled that it was time to leave his elegant hotel suite.

'Even if I'm not to know your names,' the Prime Minister said, 'I want to say thank you for the work that you do. You know that I'm serious about the possibility that the conference could end in a war between some of the greatest countries in the world. It would be such a global disaster that it may turn into World War Three. If . . .' The Prime Minister hesitated. 'If anyone was left to speak of it afterwards.'

KEEPING SECRETS

Once the Prime Minister had left them, walking briskly into the adjoining room to receive a call on his mobile phone, the Squad made to leave, eyeing the ropes still dangling on the balcony outside. But Julia stopped them.

'Wait,' she said. 'There's more.'

Kester, Lily, Adnan and Hatty moved into a tight cluster round their commander.

'As you know, I am leaving Tromsø tonight,' Julia said. 'There are to be no adults here other than those strictly involved in the conference. You'll be working alone, but I'll remain mission commander . . . from a distance. So, before I go: any questions?'

'Who are we looking for?' Hatty asked, putting her hands on her hips. 'And also why didn't you want to talk about suspects in front of the Prime Minister?'

Julia rolled her eyes. 'Hatty, Hatty, Hatty . . .'

'Yes, Julia?'

'Your mind never rests, does it?'

'Never,' Hatty replied.

'OK.' Julia smiled, looking at her watch. 'I'll tell you. The first person is a Russian. He's called Sergei Esenin. His father was a well-known spy.'

'And you think he's a spy too?' Adnan jumped in.

'We have no direct evidence that Esenin junior is a secret agent. That's what we want you to discover,' Julia said brusquely, checking her watch again. 'The fact is that he's here and, if he is a spy, or some sort of undercover operative, we need you to get evidence to prove it. But he has the credentials to be a genuine expert on oil drilling in the Arctic. It is possible he's not a spy and never has been. OK?'

'OK,' Hatty said. 'Who's the other suspect?'

'An American,' Julia answered.

'And what do we know about him?' Kester asked.

'He's a major political figure. He's great friends with the President of the USA and . . .'

Hatty closed her eyes. '. . . and with our new friend the Prime Minister?' she suggested.

'Yes, Hatty. With the Prime Minister.'

'Which is why you made Hatty keep her mouth shut in front of him,' Adnan added.

'Yes.' Julia stood and began to button up her coat. 'His name is Frank Hawk.'

'I read about him on the flight over here,' Lily cut in. 'He's an oil man and has made billions from selling oil. He's on the US negotiating team for this conference. He lives for oil.'

'He does,' Julia agreed.

'So he's going to be all for saving the polar bears then?' Adnan said.

Julia shook her head. 'In fact, he argues that there's no such thing as global warming. He says it's been made up.'

'What?' Adnan shouted. 'Is he stupid?'

'On the contrary,' Julia said. 'He knows exactly what he's doing. He makes money out of oil, therefore he's never going to admit that using it causes the Arctic ice to melt.'

'How does he know the Prime Minister?' Kester asked.

'Good question, Kester.'

'But what's the answer?' Hatty pressed.

'They were introduced by the American President. They went shooting together.'

'Shooting?'

'Yes.'

'Shooting what?'

'I don't know. Birds? Deer?'

'Urghh,' Adnan said.

'Exactly,' Lily agreed. 'How can anyone shoot a deer, let alone eat one? I used to see them in the hills all the time where I grew up in Yorkshire. They're beautiful animals.'

'Well, just remember to go carefully when you're investigating him,' Julia warned. 'If anyone's going to work out that this football tournament is a ruse to allow us to spy on the conference, then it's Frank

Hawk. Find out everything you can: but give him nothing.'

After they'd said goodbye to Julia, the children radioed Lesh, who had been waiting on the roof, monitoring the surrounding area. Once they had the all-clear, they climbed back up their ropes to be reunited with their friend, who had already found some recent images of Frank Hawk and Sergei Esenin on his SpyPad, a computer device he used for research while he was on the move, having listened in on their conversation. Now they knew what their two targets looked like.

'Quite a job we've just been given,' Lesh said, after the others had quickly briefed him.

'Yes.' Kester nodded. 'We'd better get started.'

BOYS V. GIRLS

Kester led three members of the Squad on a training run up a steep hill on the other side of the fjord from Tromsø. He wanted to get their bodies moving after the two flights from England and endless hours in airport departure lounges. He also wanted the Squad to talk – in private – now that they knew the nature of their mission.

Lesh had stayed in the hotel, researching, planning and fine-tuning their devices. Since his accident, he'd focused more on supporting the Squad's technical abilities, working on their equipment to make sure they could respond quickly to danger and communicate properly. As a result, he was more valuable to the team than ever.

Kester had announced that the run was a race.

Girls v. boys.

The hill was steep, so they ran at a slow and steady pace to cope with the incline and the loose, wet ground beneath their feet. But Lily and Hatty were soon in the lead.

As they climbed, Kester became more and more thrilled by the scenery around them, making him forget the effort his body was putting in. The city of Tromsø was attractive enough on its own, but the views around it were something else. Steep slopes. Snowfields. Smashed rocks. Twisting fjords. Layer after layer of fading mountains.

The city looked small now that they had climbed a few hundred metres, dwarfed by its dramatic setting. Kester realized that, although Tromsø was a safe and pleasant place, it was on the edge of a vast and dangerous Arctic wilderness, uninhabitable to humans. He understood that even a day out in that wilderness could prove fatal.

Kester ran alongside Adnan. The two girls were up ahead and he was glad to have the chance to talk to his friend alone. There was something other than the mission they needed to discuss. Something personal.

The five children of the Squad had been friends since they were babies. Their parents had worked with each other and socialized and gone on holiday together too.

But one terrible day – on a joint family holiday – their mums and dads had been murdered in a terrorist attack. Their parents had all been spies for the government. They had stuck together and trusted each other. They thought they'd found a safe place to have family holidays. But they were wrong.

The five were all only children and, normally, they would have been taken into care. But the children chose another path: to follow their parents' line of work.

As spies.

But now something had changed for Adnan. Something big. He had the chance of a family again. His father's brother had travelled from Pakistan, looking for his nephew – and last summer, after their last mission, he had found him. So now Adnan had a choice to make. A choice between continuing life as a child spy – or giving it all up and going back to being part of a loving family and living again in a place he could call home.

'Have you thought about it?' Kester asked, trying to regulate his breathing.

'Nothing else.' Adnan grinned, wheezing.

'I'm not surprised,' Kester said.

Adnan tried to smile.

'What did Julia say?' panted Kester, seeing that the girls were stretching their lead. They knew about Adnan's dilemma and were gutted at the prospect of losing another member of the Squad, but respected the fact that he didn't seem to want to talk about it a lot with everyone.

'She said it was up to me,' Adnan gasped, wiping a sweatband across his forehead.

'And?' Kester asked, noticing that, for once, Adnan was not trying to be funny, but actually having a proper conversation.

'I know my uncle. We met a few times when I was a kid. And I got on really well with my cousins the last time I saw them,' Adnan panted, in between the deep breaths he needed to take to keep running. 'They're well-off. It would be a good life.'

'But?' Kester pressed his friend. He could sense a hesitancy in his voice. 'Why aren't you jumping at the chance?'

'I don't know. I love this life. Being a spy. Our missions. Our friendship. Isn't this what all children dream of? A life like this? But the chance to be with family again . . . even if it's not my mum and dad . . .'

Adnan's voice tailed off and Kester didn't push him. He was trying to think anyway. It was hard to imagine what Adnan was going through. He wondered how he would feel if he was offered the chance of living in a house with adults and children who loved him. The chance of coming down to breakfast and putting on the TV football highlights in his pyjamas. The normal things most children take for granted. Birthdays. Holidays. Easter. Christmas.

And then he was hit by a memory. Deep down. Ever since Kester's own parents had died, all he'd been able to think about was *that* day, the way they'd died, the feeling of loss, the things he wished he'd not said to them. But now, seeping through, was a good memory.

Christmas.

Laughing with his mum.

A Christmas tree.

Presents.

Nice food.

Playing on the Wii with his dad.

Kester stopped running and put his hands on his knees. He was stunned. This was a *good* memory from his life before. The first one, after all this time. He felt like crying, or laughing. He wasn't sure which.

'I'm going to make a decision after this mission,' Adnan confessed. 'Julia asked that I do that at least. But first we have a job to do.'

Kester nodded.

'After this, I decide.'

'Good idea,' Kester said.

Ten minutes later, the four children were at the top of the mountain, looking across miles and miles of wooded hillsides, snowfields and, in the distance, the range of sharp black mountains that they'd seen from the roof of the hotel. Kester chose a spot next to a noisy stream for their conversation.

No one had said a word about the details of their mission or the Prime Minister since they'd left Tromsø. But now they could talk.

'I thought he was nice,' Lily began.

'The Prime Minister?' Kester asked.

'Yes.'

'Hmmmm,' Hatty said.

'What?' Lily asked.

'He's a politician,' Hatty went on. 'He's supposed to seem nice.'

Lily's face clouded slightly because she was remembering mistakes she'd made in trusting people before.

One person.

The commander on their last mission.

Jim.

And how he'd betrayed them.

They'd been in Poland, working under Jim, who was a former England footballer and British spy. He'd directed their mission and sent them into three dangerous situations, the last one ending with the England team football nearly being blown up, the children's lives in terrible danger and Lesh breaking his back.

Lily cleared her mind of dark thoughts.

'Maybe you're right,' she said. 'We can't really trust anyone.'

Kester shook his head. 'No, the Prime Minister *is* nice. He's trying to stop World War Three. That's a good thing, isn't it?'

Lily shrugged.

There was a long silence which Kester chose to fill. 'Not everyone's like Jim, Lily. Jim was a double agent. He betrayed us. The Prime Minister's OK. Julia trusts him.'

'She trusted Jim too, didn't she?'

'We should move on,' Hatty said. 'Talk about *this* mission. Not the last one.'

Kester nodded. 'That's right. We have our brief from Julia and the Prime Minister. We need to decide who's doing what. I think we should split into two teams. One to cover the American, the other the Russian. And, if we get spotted, then we can switch targets. Hatty with Adnan. Me with Lily.'

'And Lesh coordinates from Tromsø?' Hatty added.

Everyone nodded.

'Lesh is working on our comms now. He'll have them ready for this evening, when all the politicians go to dinner. Then we break into the American's and Russian's rooms and leave some bugs.'

'But we've got football training first,' Adnan said.

The four of them looked down the hill, through the trees, following the line of the stream. At the foot of the hill was a small football stadium with a rectangle of bright green.

The TUIL Arena, home ground of Tromsdalen FC.

'How long to get down there?' Hatty asked.

'Twenty minutes,' Kester said. 'The Canadians have the pitch now. We have it from three till five. Then the USA have it afterwards.'

'We'd better get down there,' Lily said. 'We don't want to be late for Rio. He would *not* be pleased . . .'

On the other side of the fjord back in Tromsø, alone in one of the hotel conference rooms, a man was sitting at his laptop computer viewing images of a large wooden container being loaded on to a fishing vessel.

He smiled.

The container was no ordinary cargo. It was something that had gone missing decades ago, when he had been a much younger man. Something he'd been keeping safe all this time. Now, however, was the moment to bring it to Tromsø and unleash it. But of course he'd be long gone by then.

He did not want to be in Tromsø when the forgotten nuclear warhead went off, levelling the city and rendering thousands of square miles of the Arctic uninhabitable for decades, free to be drilled for oil and gas by those who were willing to take the risk.

TEAM SPIRIT

After five minutes of stretches on the AstroTurf of the TUIL Arena, the England youth team captain, Rio, asked his teammates to run round the perimeter of the pitch. A steady pace on the lengths, then sprints on the widths.

With adults being banned from the team hotel, it had been decided that Rio would act as coach for this tournament. And he relished his role. It was a new experience for him.

Rio was tall, black and lean. He was the best player in the team by a long way. Everyone respected him. Even Hatty. Because of that respect, Hatty went at the training hard from the first minute. She loved training almost as much as playing matches. She believed in giving a hundred per cent at all times.

She also loved being a spy.

Hatty had known what her mum's job was all along and it had always been her ambition to be a spy too. But she never expected that her cover story would be so much fun. Her mum's cover had been as a telephone engineer. Not that exciting! Which is why Hatty was so happy to pretend to be a member of a youth football team, representing England.

It was almost perfect.

Except for one person.

Georgia.

As Hatty eased down from a sprint to a jog, she saw Georgia's blonde ponytail come bouncing alongside her and she knew that the other girl was about to say her piece. Georgia always had to say her piece: she was one of those people who wanted to be at the centre of things or else wanted to tear them down. Hatty accelerated, trying to avoid her rather than get involved in another argument. But that was not going to happen this time.

'What were you doing running up that hill?' Georgia gasped, trying to keep up.

Hatty didn't answer straight away. She was surprised that anyone had seen them. 'Training,' she replied.

'We're training *now*. Why do you and Kester and Adnan and Lily always have to do *extra* training?'

'We missed a training session yesterday,' Hatty explained, quick as a beat. 'You were here the day before. We were just trying to keep up with you, Georgia.'

The two girls arrived at the corner flag and Hatty set off at a fast pace, leaving Georgia behind. Why, she asked herself, did she find Georgia so difficult to deal with? Yes, Georgia was annoying, but Hatty could normally deal with annoying people all day long. With Georgia it was different.

She speeded up, feeling the other girl's eyes on her back.

After the stretching and the running, Rio set up a seven-a-side game. He preferred training to be made up mostly of short games rather than just practising football drills.

He also had a word with Lesh, who was waiting on the sidelines. Lesh had a new role in the team. He'd been a decent defender before his accident. So now he was Mr Tactics, having found some Dutch football software that helped him to analyse the team's performance and what each player was achieving on the pitch.

Almost as soon as the seven-a-side started, Lily went in hard with a tackle on Finn, one of Rio's best friends.

'Calm down, Lily,' Rio said. 'This is just a practice game.'

Lily climbed to her feet and put her hand out to Finn. He took it and let himself be pulled up by her.

'Sorry, Finn,' she said.

Finn just scowled in response.

Hatty smiled as she tracked back to cover the free kick that Lily had given away. Lily was a good footballer, a precise defender who made perfect use of space, skilfully distributing the ball. But she was also a player with aggression. Hatty loved the way people never expected that from Lily, even people who knew her. She was pretty and sweet and kind and she always had a smile on her face. But on the pitch she was a tough tackler. Hard as nails.

'What is it?' Georgia asked.

'What is what?'

'Why are you smiling? And what is it about you and Lily? And the others. You're always going off on your own. There's something weird about you.'

Hatty turned to face her enemy. 'Could it be because we're mates?'

'No.'

'Honestly?'

'No.'

'What then?' Hatty asked, slightly worried that Georgia was asking too many questions and how it could make trouble for them, especially as they had to get away sharpish after training to plant listening devices and track their targets in the conference hotel.

'There's something else,' Georgia said as if to herself. 'I'll find out. It's just a matter of time.'

LISTENING DEVICES

Lesh wheeled himself across the hotel's vast lobby area as men in black suits and women in long dresses walked towards the bar, to drink and be entertained by a children's string quartet. Lesh could barely hear their music for the noise of talking and laughter.

The hotel was something else. The reception area was massive. An elegant wooden staircase at the side. A deep red carpet. Gold painted furniture. Dozens of shimmering chandeliers. Through a double doorway to the left there was a huge banqueting suite laid out with fancy cutlery and wine glasses. Seven o'clock in the evening and the Arctic Conference was hosting its first dinner.

Perfect, Lesh thought. Now the Squad would have free run of the hotel to track everyone they needed to and stop them doing whatever they were planning to do to start a war. He turned his wheelchair swiftly and headed for the lifts.

Lesh allowed five adults to come out of a lift before he wheeled himself in. A man with short blond hair held the door for him, smiling kindly. Lesh smiled back. Then the lift doors closed, leaving Lesh on his own in a small over-lit space, a large mirror to his left, the reflection of a boy in a wheelchair staring back at him.

Lesh hated lifts now. First, they were a reminder that he couldn't climb staircases and he therefore depended on them. Second, the way they moved swiftly up or down brought on the feeling he'd had when he'd fallen down the church tower in Poland. The helplessness. The fear. He felt all that now, but knew that if he closed his eyes and gritted his teeth until his jaw hurt he'd be OK.

Two minutes later, Lesh was in room 312. His room. Where he'd arranged to meet the other four Squad members.

'You're in charge, Lesh,' Kester announced.

Lesh nodded. Kester, their leader, was allowing Lesh to lead this stage of the operation because he was the expert on the devices they were about to use. That made Lesh feel good. It meant he was a valuable member of the team, something he had been worried he would no longer be after his accident.

'We've got two hours to get into the two targets' rooms. Kester and Lily will go into Frank Hawk's, the American. Hatty and Adnan into Esenin's, the Russian. You've all got your radios, so we can stay in contact. I'll monitor you from here. Your job is to plant these.'

Lesh took out a small wallet the size of a DS or a PSP. Inside were six small pins with minute glassy heads on the end. As he did so, he was pleased to see the other Squad members check their earpieces and the mics in their watches. Routine practice before a mission.

'These,' Lesh said with a smile, 'are the new cameras.'

'Seriously?' Adnan asked.

'Seriously,' Lesh said. 'If you put the sharp end into the corner of a piece of furniture, this camera can film a whole room. I'm using the CCTV cameras too. I've been monitoring them for an hour. Everyone on the hotel guest list has left floors five and six for the dining area. All the rooms are empty. That's what the conference organizers agreed.'

'OK,' Hatty said.

'The only hard bit is getting the cameras where we need them. So make sure they all have a good view of the room. Somewhere high. Maybe in a doorway. Can you do that?'

'Yes,' Kester said, followed by the others.

'Good. Once you've put the camera in position, you need to activate it by twisting it a quarter turn clockwise. Don't forget.'

'We won't.'

'OK,' Lesh said, 'I want you all in the stairways for when I give you the all-clear to go in.'

*

Kester and Lily waited in the breezeblock stairwell for just two minutes before they heard Lesh's voice on the radio. 'Go in. All clear.'

They walked down the carpeted corridor, approaching room 615. Kester placed a plastic card on the pad beneath the door handle – a duplicate key Lesh had made for them – and pushed the door open.

Frank Hawk's room.

Once inside, they closed the door quickly behind them and took in a king-size double bed, a huge wooden desk, lamps, gold-and-cream wallpaper. A tray with a half-drunk bottle of red wine.

Kester knew he was supposed to feel nervous doing jobs like this. They were in someone's room without permission after all. Frank Hawk might be aggressive or dangerous and could come back at any moment. But Kester actually enjoyed the feeling. Maybe it was because he knew that the chances of someone actually coming back were low, what with Lesh covering them and dinner having only just begun.

Lily planted the camera in the top corner of a doorway, away from the door itself. Pressed deep into the wood so that it seemed invisible.

'Good.' Kester grinned. 'Shall we check the room for documents? We've got time.'

Lily was about to reply when they both heard Lesh's alarmed voice on the radio. 'Abort. A man

– I think it's Hawk – coming down the corridor. From nowhere.'

Kester and Lily felt their hearts sink, their breathing quicken. There was no *time* to abort. They looked for places to hide. Behind curtains. Under beds. Anywhere.

Then a noise in the corridor. A handle turning. The door easing open.

Kester dropped to the floor behind the sofa, next to Lily, in possibly the worst hiding place they'd ever found themselves in.

WARHEAD

Kester and Lily crouched motionless behind the sofa in Frank Hawk's room, their eyes locked on each other as they listened to someone enter, pick something off the floor, then cough.

A man's cough.

Kester cursed the fact that he had not activated the spy camera. If he had, Lesh would have been able to tell them what the man was doing and where – exactly – he was. But, for now, he and Lily knew nothing.

Then they heard the sound of a zip opening or closing on a bag or a jacket, followed by a plastic popping noise.

Kester tried to work out what he was hearing. Was Hawk pulling a gun out of the bag? Did he keep the bullets in some kind of plastic pouch? He was thinking about the worst possible thing it could be, because he knew he had to be ready for whatever happened.

The next sound they heard gave them an answer to exactly what was going on. Two short bursts of a hissing sound. Kester smiled at Lily and tapped his armpit, to indicate the American was using an aerosol can. Lily smiled too. He wasn't here to catch them in the act of spying: he'd come back to his room merely to spray on some deodorant and he didn't know two children were crouched behind his fancy sofa.

Now if he would only just go!

Lily and Kester kept quiet as tiny particles of the spray that Frank Hawk had used on his armpits drifted over them both, illuminated by the light streaming in through the window. Lily tried not to breathe in, for fear of sneezing or coughing. Soon the door handle rattled as if it was being opened again and the door slammed.

Kester counted to ten before looking. It was always possible that the man had pretended to close the door and leave, but was, in fact, standing there with a gun aimed at the two of them, ready to blow their heads off.

Next Kester took his SpyPhone out of his pocket and – using the screen as a makeshift mirror – pointed it at the doorway.

Nobody there.

He looked round the corner of the sofa to confirm.

'Clear,' he whispered.

Lily frowned. 'That was close.'

Kester walked over to the bathroom doorway and twisted the spy camera he'd placed there.

A voice came into both their ears at once. Lesh on the radio. 'That's activated now. All clear in the corridor. Target is in the lift, going down. Extract.'

Kester and Lily left swiftly, using not the lift but the cold stairwell again, then back into the corridors of the second floor. They saw no one as they walked. No staff. No guests. No Prime Ministers.

To room 312.

Opening the door of room, they saw the other three staring back at them.

'We don't have much time,' Lesh said as soon as the door was shut. 'I'm sorry. I have no idea where Hawk came from. He didn't show up on the stairs or in the lifts. I can't make sense of it.'

'It doesn't matter, Lesh,' Kester said.

'Maybe . . .' Lesh hesitated. 'Anyway, the cameras you've all fixed are working and I have both men's rooms on my monitor.'

'Did it go OK in Esenin's room, Hatty?' Kester asked.

'Well, we were undisturbed,' Hatty replied. 'Thankfully. We planted the bug in the top of the door frame. Then we looked for papers and anything else we could find.'

'And we found something,' Adnan interrupted eagerly.

'What?' Lesh asked.

'A file with three photographs inside,' Hatty said.

'Adnan made a copy of all the images on his SpyPhone. Look.'

Adnan held his phone out to the others. They saw three images. One of a tall, cone-shaped device half buried in ice. Another of some sort of large snowmobile. Finally, a map of some islands.

'What are they?' Kester asked.

'The last is a naval chart,' Hatty said. 'Of here.'

'Here?'

'Look,' Hatty pointed. 'This is the channel where Tromsø is. The bridges on either side of this island are marked. It's the view we all saw from the hill and from the plane. But this chart shows the depth of the water across the channel. It's for ships to use to navigate through the islands, so they don't run aground.'

'What about the other pictures?' Adnan asked.

'That looks . . .' Lesh said, gesturing for a closer look. 'The conical thing, I mean. That looks like a warhead.'

'A warhead?' The other four spoke at the same time.

'A nuclear warhead,' Lesh explained. 'The part of a nuclear missile that has the bomb in it. You know, the pointed bit on the end. But it's not a modern one, it's an old one. From the 1960s.'

'How do you know that?' Adnan asked.

'I've read about them.'

'About bombs from years ago?' Adnan was surprised.

'But what's this got to do with anything *now*?' Kester challenged. 'Fifty years later.'

'The question is: what has the warhead got to do with the map?' Lesh said.

The room went quiet. Everyone racking their brains.

Kester broke the silence. 'We can work it out later,' he urged. 'The thing now is to gather evidence while everyone's up and about. We need to watch Hawk and Esenin. We need to see who they talk to. Try and hear what they talk about. Anything we can pick up tonight we can use to work out what these charts and the warhead mean. Come on.'

Kester was on his feet. 'We'll all go down to the bar area. Just hang out with the others. But try to take in as much as you can. OK?'

Lily, Hatty and Adnan all stood up and Lesh moved his wheelchair forward. They were ready.

And there was no time to lose.

THE HAWK

Lily sat with Lesh in the cafe at the side of the hotel foyer, which gave them a great view of the bar and the door through to the banqueting suite, from where the politicians were emerging. They also had a good view of the entrance to the hotel with its two revolving doors.

The other three Squad members were in the games room on the far side of the bar, pretending to play pool, but in reality watching, listening, gathering evidence.

They'd all been in position for nearly half an hour and had seen several important people standing in groups. Norwegians. Russians. Americans. People they'd researched since arriving in Norway. Also several small groups of young footballers in their national tracksuits, a stark contrast to the adults in dinner jackets and long dresses.

'I do think we need to spend more time with the rest of the team,' Lesh said. 'If we don't, they'll get suspicious. Hatty is already worried about Georgia asking questions.'

'I know,' Lily said. 'She told me. You're right, we should . . . what is it?'

Lesh had tapped his lips twice, a signal to Lily.

Something behind her. That she was not to look.

She switched instantly to normal conversation. 'So, what should we go and see tomorrow? That museum in Tromsø? It's called Polaria, isn't it?'

'Yes,' Lesh answered. 'That sounds interesting.'

'Excuse me?' The voice came from behind Lily. An American voice. Lesh was smiling up at whoever it was, so Lily turned to look at him.

And there he was.

Frank Hawk.

The American they had been tasked to monitor.

'Hi,' said Lily.

'Hi,' Hawk replied. 'Listen. Do you kids mind if I join you for a minute?'

'Sure.' Lily smiled and pulled a seat out for the American. But she could feel her heart fluttering nervously.

'I'm Frank,' the man said. 'I just saw you and . . . well, you reminded me of my grandkids back in the US. How old are you? Thirteen? Fourteen?'

'Thirteen,' Lesh answered.

The man leaned in conspiratorially and Lily and Lesh could see his greying hair and sprouting eyebrows close up. He looked a very fit and strong man for his age.

'All this adult talk gets a bit boring,' Frank Hawk

said. 'It makes you miss your family back home, so when I saw you I thought I'd come and say hi.'

'What are your grandchildren called?' Lily asked.

'Mitch and Lena,' Hawk replied, smiling like he really did miss them. 'Listen, can I get you kids a drink? Two Cokes?'

'Thanks,' Lily and Lesh said together.

The American stood and took his jacket off, putting it over the chair, then placed his hat on the table in front of them before heading over to the cafe.

'Funny – he seems quite nice,' Lesh said.

'True,' Lily agreed, slipping a tiny bugging device the size of a pin into the lip of the American's hat. 'Even though he's a global warming denier.'

Lesh supressed a laugh. Lily grinned and glanced over at the other three. She was pleased to see that they were talking to the other England players. It made them seem like they were more part of the team. They didn't need suspicious questions like Georgia's on top of trying to concentrate on the mission and playing football. Hatty was with Rio. The rest had their backs to her. Apart from Kester, who glanced back at Lily without changing his expression.

Suddenly the American was coming back with two cans of Coke.

'So tell me,' he said, 'what brings you to Norway? You're English, right?'

'Yes, we're English,' Lesh said. 'We're with the

England youth team in a football tournament. We're playing Canada, the USA and Norway.'

'Yes, I know about that,' the American said. 'I'm looking forward to those soccer games. Hoping to see the USA win. But,' he went on with a smile, 'you don't like it being called *soccer*, do you?'

Lily laughed. 'If that's what you call it, it's fine.'

'Good,' the American said, turning to Lesh. 'Can I ask about you, son? You're in the wheelchair. How do you have a role in the team? If you don't mind me asking.'

'I don't mind,' Lesh said, feeling good that the American was comfortable talking about his wheelchair: so many English people were too embarrassed to mention it. 'I *was* in the team, but I had an accident earlier this year. Now I help with the coaching. Stuff like that.'

'Good man,' the American said. 'You sound like the kind of guy I'd like to have on my team. Never give up.'

Lesh grinned. Hawk seemed OK. So much so that it felt strange fishing for information, treating him like a possible enemy.

'Are you here for the conference?' Lily asked Hawk, testing to see how much information he might give away.

'I am. I'm with the US party. Do you know all about the conference?' Hawk asked, looking surprised.

'A little bit,' Lily improvised, trying to stay in

character. 'Someone explained to us who all the men in suits were. We knew you weren't here for the tournament!'

Hawk laughed. 'True. Well, I'm here campaigning for my country. It's not easy. So many countries arguing about who owns what under the ice. Especially the Russians. But better to talk like this than have a war about it, eh?'

'I understand,' Lily said. 'Do you think you'll all agree on the best thing?'

'I do,' the American said, glancing round the room. 'There are difficulties, but we'll work it out. For your generation. For you and my grandkids, eh?' He paused again and looked at his watch. 'You know, talking to you kids makes me want to call them. They'll be home from school now.'

The American lifted his jacket off the back of his chair and took his hat from the table. 'I'm gonna take a walk by the water. Call home. Listen, it's been lovely talking to you kids.'

When the American had gone, Adnan, Kester and Hatty came over to the cafe, leaving Rio and Johnny standing near the lifts.

'What was that all about?' Hatty asked.

Lily answered because Lesh was tuning in to the tracking device she'd slipped into Frank Hawk's hat. She explained what had been said.

'He was nice,' she finished.

'Hmmmm,' Hatty said.

'No, he really did seem . . .'

Lesh held his hand up for silence so that he could hear the American well. 'He's talking to his grandkids,' he said. 'Asking them about their schoolwork, stuff like that.'

'Seems like a normal man,' Adnan suggested.

'What did *you* make of him?' Kester asked Lesh in a low voice.

'Friendly. Generous. Family man. Proud to be American. Like I said, a nice person. But he could still be the most evil man on the planet, I suppose.'

Two hours later, back in Lesh's room, the Squad were planning the next day, when Lesh, listening in, reported that the American was talking on his phone again. This time from his room. Everyone went quiet to allow him to listen. They watched Lesh's expression drop from an interested smile to a deep frown. No one spoke when he put the headphones down.

'He's just called the White House,' Lesh explained.

'And?' Hatty asked.

'And he was talking to the President about a warhead, I think. A missing warhead. That there's a threat . . . a possible threat to this conference. But that he doesn't know how it will be delivered or by who. But that he thinks it's the Russians.'

TUESDAY

ATTACK

Morning in the Arctic Circle and the sun was already above the mountains, creating a low light that glittered off the fjords. But a keen, cool breeze took the edge off any warmth. The temperature had dropped overnight, colder air moving in from the north.

Most of the England youth team were gathered in the hotel foyer, all in tracksuits with their kitbags in a pile against one of the walls, waiting for the bus that was due to take them over to the stadium. And the game against Canada.

Georgia and two of the boys were missing. After a few minutes, Rio snapped.

'Right. I'll go and find them. I'll see you in ten minutes. Here. Then we go. OK?'

The rest of the team nodded and began to disperse. To the cafe. To the toilets.

The Squad members drifted off too, deliberately one by one, making their way past UN soldiers who were stationed outside the hotel, guarding the conference. But soon the Squad were together again, gathered in a circle at the edge of the fjord by the conference hotel, next to a barrier made up of metre-high pieces of concrete that had been slotted together to protect the hotel from terrorist attack. The noises from the fjord and the air-conditioning units were useful: no one would be able to listen in on the Squad there.

A fishing boat had come in close to the hotel. The five kept a careful eye on it as a row erupted between the captain and a blue-bereted UN soldier.

'Come on,' Kester said. 'We're playing the Canada game in a couple of hours. But before that let's review the mission. We have five minutes before Rio comes back. What do we know?'

'Last night we discovered that the Russians, maybe Esenin, could be in possession of a warhead and bringing it here. Maybe . . .'

'Maybe,' repeated Lesh.

'But it looks like a credible threat,' Kester said.

'Very credible,' Lesh agreed. 'And one we have to pursue. I've found out more about Esenin, who has to be our prime suspect for this line of enquiry. His father used to be in the army and the FSB – that's the Russian Secret Service. But there's no record of Sergei being involved. He seems to be on a one-man mission to forge a way for Russia and Europe to peacefully find oil and gas together.'

'Sounds like a convenient front,' Hatty said. 'It's highly likely that he's pretending. Don't we know that now? After what we found in his room. The images of the warhead. The maps. Everything to do with his father.'

'Perhaps,' Lily said. 'But bear in mind they might have been planted in his room. It's unlikely, but we can't rule it out.'

'Esenin is our number-one suspect,' Kester said, looking at the fishing boat in the foreground, almost touching the harbour wall, the captain and now three UN soldiers shouting at each other. 'But we have to follow up the other leads. Lily's right.'

'What about Frank Hawk then?' Adnan asked.

'He's everything he said he was last night,' Lesh replied. 'He's got grandkids the same age as us. He used to be a politician. Now he gives talks about how drilling for oil and using it doesn't create global warming. He's also a director of several businesses. And he likes sports.'

'What sort of sports?' Lily asked, watching a girl about their age who was standing on the far side of the fishing boat.

'Baseball's his favourite. Shooting. Soccer,' Lesh answered.

'Soccer?' Kester muttered.

'Soccer.' Lesh smiled. He knew Kester hated the word. 'That's football to you and me.'

Kester screwed up his face.

Then Lily interrupted. 'I don't get it,' she said. 'How can he be a loving granddad and not believe in global warming? Everybody knows about the ice melting and the polar bears losing their habitat. He must worry about the world his grandchildren will grow up in if global warming isn't stopped.'

But, before any of the others had a chance to respond, their voices were drowned out by a violent crashing, hissing sound.

Lesh wheeled himself backwards as the other Squad members dropped to the floor to take cover behind the concrete barriers, all braced for what sounded like some sort of attack. They'd been trained for this.

One. Protect themselves.

Two. Analyse the situation.

Three. Decide how to act.

The Squad watched in horror as the top part of one side of the fishing boat they'd seen docking blew outwards, a wall of foaming water cascading across the harbour and towards the foyer of the hotel.

Immediately, alarms went off and UN soldiers sprinted towards the scene, while other people ran in the opposite direction. There was water everywhere.

'Do we act?' Hatty shouted to Kester.

Kester glanced over the barriers. In a second he took in the scene. It was strange. It had looked and sounded like a bomb, but there were no casualties, no fire, no smoke. Just a lot of water that was now flooding the hotel entrance.

'Negative,' Kester said. 'Not as the Squad. There are plenty of UN soldiers to deal with it. This is no bomb. It's just water. No explosives. But we need to get close. Let's run up to try to help. Like we're just . . . you know . . . kids. Agreed?'

The children moved towards the hotel entrance. As they did, Lily took in several things. The huge amount of water pouring off the harbour. The bewildered look of several conference delegates as they comforted each other following the shock, their shoes and trouser bottoms soaked.

And that girl – about their age – still there, filming the whole scene. The only person not moving to or from the source of the crisis.

Lily, like the others, had been trained to notice unusual behaviour. Most days someone taking pictures in a beautiful setting would be normal. But – during what seemed to be some sort of attack or accident – the girl's behaviour stood out.

As the panic grew on the harbourside and around the hotel, Lily had to decide what to do. Their job now was to help anyone hurt, as well as gathering intelligence by being at the heart of the scene, trying to find out what was going on. A woman had been knocked over by the water and she needed help. But this girl was important.

'Lesh,' Lily whispered into her friend's ear. 'Take some images of that girl over there. She's filming everything.'

'Done,' Lesh said, holding up his SpyPad.

'Right. I'll go and have a friendly chat,' Lily added.

But, as she made to leave, there was another terrible sound, an increasing roar that distracted Lily for a second and sent everyone into a panic, running in all directions.

And Lily saw that the girl had vanished.

MILITARY RESPONSE

Even before the children had made it to the cover of the hotel entrance, the second noise spread terror across the harbour.

The air began vibrating, a *thump-thump-thump* becoming louder and louder, as four huge military helicopters appeared from behind one of the mountains, like something out of an action film.

The Squad knew immediately what this was: a major military response. The air full of choppers. A dozen armoured vehicles parked in front of the conference hotel, spilling small squads of blue-capped UN soldiers on to the surrounding streets. There was chaos and confusion everywhere, but the Squad stood firm, looking carefully around, evaluating the threat, working out what to do next.

When the noise of the helicopters and vehicles died down, they heard the announcement:

PLEASE GO TO THE MAIN CONFERENCE HALL, WHICH HAS BEEN SECURED.

PLEASE GO TO THE MAIN CONFERENCE HALL, WHICH HAS BEEN SECURED.

PLEASE GO TO THE MAIN CONFERENCE . . .

Kester ordered the Squad to head straight for the hall.

'But what if . . .' Hatty interrupted.

'What if we can find something out?' Kester countered. 'We have to appear like normal kids. We mustn't blow our cover. So just walk like everyone else to the main hall, but keep your eyes on everything. And remember it.'

Hatty nodded. She understood that Kester had made the right call.

Kester led them directly past where they had seen the water and ice spill off the boat, en route to the main hall. Everybody else was moving quickly towards the hotel entrance, stopping as if they were worried that the helicopters that were now hovering above the hotel were about to open fire on them.

'Where's that girl?' Lily asked. 'Can anyone see her?'

'No,' Lesh said. 'She's gone. But I do have photographs of her.'

'That's something,' Lily said.

'Come on,' Kester urged. 'Inside. Watch everyone. The girl might show up. Look out for people watching, not reacting like they're scared. They're the ones who might have something to do with the water attack.'

The Squad entered the hotel foyer just as Rio and most of the rest of the England team did.

'Come on!' Rio shouted. 'The main hall. Now. Those helicopters are coming.'

'Yeah, come on!' Georgia shouted. 'We're all going to get killed.'

The Squad did as Rio suggested and ran with him, allowing him to take the lead. As they ran, Kester glanced at Hatty to see her screwing up her face.

'Let them lead,' he said quietly.

'But they should know there's no threat. They're panicking.'

'It's OK. For now. Let them think it. We just need to look scared too. Or our cover will be blown.'

Hatty grimaced, but did as Kester said.

One minute later, all the children from the football teams staying at the hotel, all wearing team tracksuits, were in the main hall with dozens of men and women in smart, expensive clothes.

It was a strange sight. Each set of people was behaving like sheep, grouping in small circles, moving around, chattering. All crowded into the grand dining hall with its wood panelling and oil paintings on the walls.

In the English group, Georgia was making the most noise. 'What's going on? Look at the doors! There are armed men on all the doors. We're going to be bombed. Can you hear the planes over us?'

Hatty longed to tell Georgia that there was nothing to worry about. This was not a major attack but just a few barrels of water off a boat; the noises above were not planes about to bomb them but UN peacekeeping helicopters protecting the airspace.

'What did you see?' Hatty asked Rio, trying to sound panicked.

'Some sort of bomb on a boat. Most of us were waiting outside the main entrance to the hotel. The bus had just drawn up. We got soaked.' He pointed at his sodden trainers. 'Then the helicopters came,' Rio said. 'But it's gone quiet. Maybe the helicopters are here to protect us?'

Hatty nodded vigorously, putting her hand on their captain's arm. 'I hope you're right, Rio,' she said, trying to look like any other teenage girl would when this kind of thing was happening. As she did, she surveyed the other team members – Johnny looked pale and shaken, Finn stood with his mouth agape, and some of the others just looked genuinely scared, two of them crying.

Then a man appeared on the stage of the main hall, demanding silence.

'LADIES AND GENTLEMEN. CHILDREN. DO NOT BE ALARMED. THERE HAS BEEN

AN INCIDENT OUTSIDE THE HOTEL, BUT WE ARE SAFE. THE UNITED NATIONS SOLDIERS ARE HERE AND IN CONTROL.'

A few of the audience shouted out questions or comments. But the man carried on regardless.

'WE HAVE ARRANGED FOR COACHES TO REMOVE YOU ALL FROM THE HOTEL. YOU WILL BE TAKEN IN MAXIMUM SECURITY TO TROMSDALEN, OUR NEIGHBOURING TOWN, OVER THE WATER. THERE IS TO BE A FOOTBALL MATCH THERE IN ONE HOUR. THE FIRST GAME OF THE INTERNATIONAL TOURNAMENT.

'THE STADIUM IS A SECURE SITE. PLEASE. IT'S A SAFER PLACE THAN HERE FOR NOW. YOU WILL ALL PROCEED CALMLY. WE MUST SECURE THE HOTEL BEFORE YOUR RETURN.'

'Great,' Rio said once the announcement was made, raising his voice above those of the other people talking. 'I was afraid this was going to mean our game was off.'

Hatty looked at him and was impressed. *Rio* wasn't panicking: he was thinking about football, just as some of the others thought they were about to be attacked. He was leading them by taking their minds off the danger.

Hatty smiled. 'Come on then,' she said. 'Let's go and play football.'

BORE DRAW

Everyone staying at the hotel – the footballers *and* all those attending the conference – were evacuated across the water and secured within a ring of UN soldiers at the TUIL Stadium. This included the various prime ministers and their negotiating teams.

As the line of five luxury coaches, with armed vehicles ahead and behind, passed over the bridge, a pair of military attack helicopters hovered level with the bridge and the coaches. Adnan looked into one of the cockpits and met the eyes of the pilot and a stern look of concentration. Adnan waved and grinned until Hatty stopped him with a slap.

Behind them, Lesh was showing Lily something on his SpyPad. A film of the water attack on YouTube.

'An environmental protest group has already put it up there,' he whispered. 'Called White Fear.'

'Have you heard of them?' Lily whispered back.

'Yes,' Lesh went on. 'They're against Arctic oil

exploration. They've made a name for themselves by pulling off stunts to raise awareness of global warming.'

'It must have been that girl,' Lily said.

'What?'

'The girl with the camera, making the film. She must be one of them, surely.'

The TUIL Arena – home to Tromsdalen FC – had seating on both sides. A larger stand that could hold several hundred to the right, a smaller one to the left. Above the stands, steep mountains reached into the pale Arctic sky. A ribbon of cloud was drifting up the tight valley that led away from the fjord.

All the politicians and footballers were directed into the main stand across a muddy track. Lesh wheeled his chair to the front of the stand. The rest of the England youth team sat behind him on plastic seats.

'Can you believe what just happened at the hotel?' Georgia gasped. 'A bomb! We almost died!'

'I think we were safe,' Hatty said, aware she shouldn't appear to be too relaxed about the incident.

'What do you know about it?' Georgia asked. 'Are you an expert on explosions? I don't think so.'

Rio cut in. 'What matters is we're safe now.'

Hatty held her tongue. But inside she really wanted to put Georgia in her place.

'Are you OK?' Kester asked Rio. 'You were great back there.' He wanted their captain to know that he thought he'd done well. During their last mission, Rio had been difficult; he and Kester had not hit it off. But now they were developing respect for each other. Exactly the sort of relationship that Kester needed with the team captain.

Rio hesitated before replying, then nodded quickly.

'You were right to get us to concentrate on the football,' Kester went on. 'It helped.'

'Thanks, mate,' Rio said, looking at Kester and smiling.

When everyone was seated, a woman in a military uniform strode out on to the pitch and began to speak into a microphone. Behind her, a massive mountain rose high into the sky, covered in trees and with bare rock at its summit.

'Ladies and gentlemen and children,' the military woman addressed them in faltering English. 'I am Ana Hamsun. For security reasons we are bringing you here. Safety at the conference hotel is unclear and we bring you safely to here. But do not be alarmed. The hotel will soon be quite safe. We are making the last checks.'

'So what was the damn explosion?' a voice shouted out. Lily quickly identified the speaker as Frank Hawk.

'It is just a stunt,' Ana Hamsun replied. 'There is never any danger. We have a claim from the White

Fear, a world ecological group. They are releasing just water from their boat. No explosives. They are telling us this. It is a voice. A voice for your conference perhaps?'

As she spoke, Ana Hamsun's voice was drowned out by people arguing and some laughter.

'Now.' She raised her voice. 'We play the first soccer game of our children's Arctic tournament in no time. Canada and England. It is playing here for your relaxation. Please, stay and enjoy the game.'

'But are we free to leave?' someone asked from the back of the stadium.

Ana Hamsun frowned, then consulted a woman at her side, who spoke into a radio. The audience watched a helicopter hover over the stadium, then swing high to the top of the mountain, as they waited for an answer.

'Yes,' she said eventually. 'It is now all clear to return on the coaches to the hotel. But we would be happy if you to stay . . .'

Immediately, half the people in the stadium stood up to leave, the woman's voice drowned out by the sound of stomping boots and upturned seats.

'Great,' Adnan said. 'It's so good to see that world leaders like to support their young people and watch them play football.'

Kester thought that the match was strange from the moment it kicked off. Maybe it was because of the bomb scare or the fact that there was still a pair of armed attack helicopters patrolling the mountainsides close to the pitch, but both the England and Canada teams were showing each other a lot of respect, almost as if it would be rude to attack and score a goal.

It was all passing. Short balls through the defence and midfield. But nothing adventurous. No long balls. *Safe*, Kester thought as the first half drew to an end. *Safe and boring*.

At half-time Rio tried to use his captain's role to inspire his players. They were sitting in a cramped dressing room, with wooden benches and a tiled floor.

'I know this has been a strange day,' Rio said. 'And I know we need to keep things tight, but we also need to step up the pace, press the ball better. We're safe at the back, but there's no drive going forward. We need urgency.'

'We need better balls from the defence,' Georgia said, glaring at Hatty. 'They're just passing it about like it doesn't matter.'

'Have we let a goal in?' Hatty snapped. Georgia said nothing.

'Have we?' Still nothing.

'No,' Hatty pressed. 'We've defended and *not* let a goal in. But, tell me, have you attackers scored?'

Georgia scowled.

'No one's scored,' Rio said, trying to calm the two girls, who were off their benches now, glaring at each other across the tiles.

'So who's doing their job and who's not?' Hatty pressed.

Rio stood up and put his hands out. 'Come on, let's be a team again. That's how we work best. This is what we need to do –'

But there was no time for Rio to finish his speech as the dressing-room door burst open with a loud crack. Lesh, kicking the door open, wheeled himself in.

'That was rubbish!' he shouted. 'You should be hammering this lot.' The door slammed behind him.

'You make me sick,' he went on. 'Look at you – all of you – with your two working legs. I could do better than you crawling around on my hands and knees. Get your fingers out! And you two can stop your bickering, Hatty. Georgia. It's pathetic! You're supposed to be teammates.'

There was a long silence as the whole team looked at Lesh in guilty admission. How could they reply to that?

But Lesh was ahead of them. 'You have no idea what to say to me, do you?'

The whole team shook their heads.

'Well, I don't want to hear words. I want to see

action on the pitch. I've been analysing you. Your pass completion is poor. Especially in the last third. You've not had enough shots on goal. You're doing all the basics wrong.'

Another stunned silence.

'He's right,' Rio said quietly.

The second half was better. Far better. Thanks to Lesh's rocket.

The England team played with pace and precision, knocking the ball about at speed. The Canadian players couldn't live with it.

Rio set up the first goal. A long ball to Georgia's feet as she sprinted into the penalty area to clip it home.

1–0.

The second goal came from deep in the defence. Adnan bowled a ball out to Kester, who knocked it to Hatty. Hatty ran with it, played it wide to Johnny who, after a one-two with a teammate, crossed it on to Georgia's head.

2–0.

Although Hatty was pleased they were winning, she hated seeing Georgia score all the goals. It was just a matter of time before the other girl said something to her about it.

And she was right. After firing in a third goal, Georgia avoided the embraces of her other teammates and ran over to confront Hatty.

'Who's not doing their job now?' she shouted.

Hatty closed her eyes and counted to ten. *Remember this is a cover story*, she said to herself. *You're a spy and making Georgia think you're just an ordinary girl is part of that cover.*

'Well done, Georgia,' Hatty smiled. 'You've done brilliantly.'

Georgia shook her head. 'You don't mean that.'

'I do,' said Hatty. 'I want to win this game as much as you do. I'm sure you'd like to congratulate us defenders for not letting a goal in.'

'Not really,' Georgia laughed as the rest of the team caught up with her and jumped on her back.

Hatty was really struggling now. *Don't let her get to you. Don't let her get to you*, she was saying under her breath, over and over. She desperately needed something to take her mind off Georgia and Lily provided it.

As it was 3–0 and the game was as good as over, Canada brought on three substitutes.

'Look,' Lily said to Hatty under her breath.

'What?'

'Canada's number sixteen.'

It was a girl, aged about thirteen, dark hair, strikingly beautiful.

'The girl from the harbour. The one who was filming,' said Lily. 'Those films she took: they must be the ones that are on the Internet already. And you know that an environmental group – White Fear – is claiming credit for the films. That must mean she's involved.'

'But she's a footballer,' Hatty said as Adnan joined them.

'And there's no way anyone could be a footballer and a spy, is there?' Adnan added.

'Very helpful, Adnan. Lily, tell Kester. We need to have a word with that girl after the game. I'll just go and update Lesh.' Hatty jogged over to Lesh, who handed her a bottle of water.

'What is it?' he said quietly.

'That number sixteen. She's the girl from the fishing boat earlier,' Hatty said. 'Didn't you get a photo of her?'

'Yes.'

'Can you do some face recognition? Quickly.'

'Consider it done,' Lesh said. 'I'll find out everything I can.'

INUIT

Tromsdalen Football Club hosted a party after the game, for the teams that took part and for the crowd who had stayed. It was held in a large room underneath the main stand, a row of white-cloth-covered tables running along one of the walls, bearing food and drink.

Once changed, the England team joined everybody else. Hatty, Lily and Adnan ahead. Kester wheeling Lesh in through the bottom of the stand, keeping back so they could talk. They both looked out towards the city to see that the impressive security operation was ongoing. A perimeter of armed vehicles was still there, along with dozens of troops.

'Is she still here?' Kester muttered, leaning into Lesh.

'I didn't see her leave,' Lesh said. 'I stayed outside to check.'

As they entered the function room, Kester stood on tiptoe to look round the room.

But it was Lesh who saw her first. 'There she is,'

he spoke quietly into his mic. 'Far corner. Underneath the stone steps. On her own.'

Hatty and Adnan – who were wired up to Lesh – saw the girl and walked across the room to intercept her as she started to move towards the door. They needed to find out who she was and why she'd been filming just as the attack took place. Of course they couldn't ask her directly, but they *could* find out more about her.

Kester spoke into his mic as he walked. 'Anything coming up on face recognition, Lesh?'

'She doesn't come up as known on the system,' Lesh reported as Hatty and Adnan closed in on her. 'But what I can tell you is that her facial features match those of a Canadian Inuit. What people used to call Eskimos. So she might have some sort of reason to be here: to protect Canada? There's every chance she's linked to White Fear. Keep that in mind.'

Hatty, now fully informed, had reached the girl.

'Hello,' the girl said in a friendly voice. 'Well done this afternoon. You were very good.'

'Thank you,' Hatty said, noticing how dark the girl's hair was and how beautiful she looked up close. Hatty was also surprised at the girl's friendliness and that she hadn't needed to engineer a conversation herself.

'I'm Katiyana,' the girl said, beaming. 'I saw you at the hotel before the accident.'

Hatty smiled now. This girl wasn't hiding anything. She'd not expected her to draw attention to that. The conversation began to feel more like a game.

'We saw you too,' Adnan cut in. 'I'm Adnan. This is Hatty. So you're from the Canada team?'

'Yes. But we did not play well today.'

'I don't think anyone did,' Adnan said. 'It's been a strange day.'

Then suddenly, and before they had the chance to talk any more, the girl's expression changed completely, from smiling and chatty to something much darker. Adnan was worried it was aimed at him. That he had said something to offend, or worse, alert her, but then he heard Lesh's voice in his earpiece.

'Frank Hawk. Right behind you, Adnan.'

It happened quickly. 'Hello, children. I'm Frank Hawk. I'm with the American negotiating team. I wanted to say thank you for the game today. It was very entertaining.'

'Thanks,' Hatty said, studying the man's short grey hair, spotting a tiny shaving cut on his neck. Why had he come over when they were all talking – just as he had with Lily and Lesh? Had he chosen that moment especially – or was it a coincidence? Did he suspect the Squad? And did that mean that they should suspect *him* of something?

'I should probably want Canada to win, being

American,' Hawk went on. 'But my great-grandfather was from England, so I was rooting for you kids today.'

Adnan nodded. The American was being friendly, but he noticed Katiyana was not.

'Well, thanks again for the entertainment, kids,' the American finished. 'Keep playing well . . . until you play the USA.'

The three children stayed quiet for a few seconds as Frank Hawk moved away to speak to some other people. Katiyana was still scowling.

'Do you know him?' Adnan asked, wanting to understand why the girl's manner had changed so dramatically.

'I know of him,' Katiyana replied. 'He's not a good man.'

'No?'

'No.'

'Why? What's he done wrong?'

'You know who he is?' the Canadian girl said after a long pause.

'No,' Hatty said. 'Should we?'

'He's Frank Hawk. He's a businessman. He likes people to think he's trying to help the world by talking at conferences, like the one they're having here. But all he's interested in is making money from his oil companies.'

'Oil?' Adnan asked, feeling Hatty elbow him in the ribs. He was showing too much specific interest.

'Yes, oil. And the more oil he drills and burns, the

more the ice melts up here – and in Canada. He says he's an expert about the Arctic. He says the ice isn't melting. He lies. I live in the Arctic. I know. He only says these things so that he can drill for more oil. He pays scientists to lie and to say that they've done experiments that prove there's no such thing as global warming.'

Lesh – who could hear the conversation in his earpiece – made mental notes. Things he wanted to find out more about. As much about the girl as Frank Hawk. She was a suspect now too.

'Have they proved that there is global warming though?' Hatty asked, trying to sound rude, so that the girl might react badly to her and give something away.

'Yes, they have. I have,' the girl said. 'I live in Nunavut in Canada. People are losing everything where I live. The ice is melting and that means the way we live and make our money is coming to an end. Our way of life is disappearing. People who say it's not true have no idea. No idea at all.'

'You sound like you'd do anything to change people's minds,' Hatty said, deliberately trying to provoke Katiyana further.

Suddenly Hatty heard a familiar voice behind her.

'Hi.' It was Rio. Rio with Finn.

'Hello.' Katiyana smiled sweetly, making her look even more beautiful than ever.

'I'm Rio. I'm the England captain.'

'I know.' Katiyana blushed. 'I saw you on the pitch. You were good.'

And Hatty realized that their conversation was over.

The five Squad members chose to walk back to the hotel from the TUIL Arena. Their route took them through a housing estate and past a modern white cathedral to the Bruvegen Bridge. They needed to go over the bridge from Tromsdalen back to Tromsø.

The air was cooling. Once they were on the bridge, the wind that passed down the channel buffeted them. A cold, icy wind. They could feel the bridge shuddering as the air currents moved around it. With no mountainsides or buildings to shield them from the Arctic weather, they were very exposed. But it was a beautiful setting, so the wind didn't worry them.

The children saw two things as they walked across the bridge. The first was a huge red-and-white boat heading in from the south, HURTIGRUTEN written on its side. As they saw it, they heard it too: its horn filled the fjords with a deep blast of sound that echoed from mountainside to mountainside.

'That's the Hurtigruten,' Lesh explained. 'It's a boat service that runs up and down the Norwegian coast. There are a few boats going north and south at any one time. It takes a week to travel the length of the country.'

The other thing they all saw from the bridge was a man standing exactly halfway across, hundreds of metres above the choppy water. And he looked familiar.

'Isn't that . . . ?' Kester asked.

'Sergei Esenin,' Lesh confirmed. 'No question. Just like he looks in the photos we saw.' 'What's he doing here?' Lily asked.

'I don't know,' Kester replied. 'But is it normal to stop on a bridge and just stare into the water?'

'Well, we're doing it,' Hatty pointed out.

'True,' Kester conceded.

The Squad carried on talking as they moved past Esenin, covering the sort of trivia they knew would sound normal. Football. Who was winning and who was losing back in England.

The Russian's eyes were so fixed on the channel of water beneath him that he didn't seem to notice them anyway. He looked young and extremely fit. Not at all how they imagined a scientist to be.

When they were safely past him, Kester asked the question everybody had lodged in their minds. 'What was he looking for?'

'Something in the water?' Lily suggested.

'Or under it?' Lesh added. 'A Russian submarine?'

'The warhead,' Hatty said. 'He knows it's coming in and he's monitoring it. Maybe.'

'I think it's time we reported back to the Prime Minister,' Kester concluded. 'We're starting to get some ideas about what's going on – and who might be involved.'

The five children picked up their pace, heading towards the conference hotel, as a vicious hailstorm swept off the mountains.

AERIAL ATTACK

The Prime Minister was already running late.

He'd been speaking on the telephone to the American President, the call running over into the time when he should have been round the table with all the representatives of the Arctic Powers.

His adviser called a lift for him, then asked, 'Shall I come down with you, sir?'

'No, it's fine, Luxton. This hotel is safer than Downing Street.'

'I could call a UN soldier?'

'Really. Don't worry. I'll be OK.'

The Prime Minister entered the lift and pressed the button to take him directly to the ground floor. The doors slid shut and he could feel the floor of the lift dropping. He'd be downstairs in seconds.

Then the lift stopped dead. The Prime Minister pressed the ground-floor button again.

Nothing.

Knowing he was vulnerable, he pressed the alarm button without hesitating.

Still nothing.

Then, to his horror, a large panel in the roof of the lift opened. The most powerful man in Britain was helpless. He could do nothing. He was unarmed and had no means of calling for help. He could only watch as a lone figure dropped to stand next to him.

'Hello, sir,' Hatty said soothingly, seeing how anxious the Prime Minister looked. 'I'm sorry to frighten you. This was really the only way.'

'I wasn't frightened,' the Prime Minister snapped.

Hatty felt like contradicting him, but knew she had to get down to business. 'I need to report to you, sir. Julia wanted us to – in person – when we had information that might help you.'

The Prime Minister nodded and straightened his tie, which didn't need straightening.

'Yes?' he said, clearly still in shock.

'We've been keeping an eye on three people,' she started.

'Three? I thought it was two.'

'It's three now, sir. The first is Esenin, the Russian. We've been into his room and found some papers. Images of a nuclear warhead and charts of the waters around Tromsø.'

'The Russians!' The Prime Minister shook his head gravely. 'Go on,' he said.

'We also saw him scanning the fjord earlier, from the Bruvegen Bridge up there.'

'And what do you think that means?'

'The warhead looks like one from the 1960s,' Hatty said. 'It's one that went missing – the Americans lost it in Greenland.'

'Lost it? I find that hard to believe.'

'Yes, sir. It's well documented.' Hatty hesitated. 'We think it's possible that he – or someone – is bringing it here to use.'

'But it's not here yet?'

'No.'

'Well, I can help with that. I can arrange for satellites to monitor the waterways around here. He'll struggle to get it in. Who are your other suspects?'

'Frank Hawk,' Hatty said, pleased the Prime Minister seemed to be relaxing and taking her seriously.

'Frank?' the PM asked. 'What about him? Are you working with him?'

'No. He's a suspect.'

'What?' The Prime Minister looked cross. 'He's not a key player here. Just an adviser to the Americans. I was just talking to the President about him. In fact, Frank has even told me he's met you kids. He likes you.'

'We like him too, sir,' Hatty said. 'But we've had some information about him and his interests. About his position against global warming. Something doesn't feel quite right. We've been into his rooms and . . .'

'His rooms? No. Why? What did you find?'

'Nothing, sir. We were nearly caught, but we, well, we hid . . .'

The Prime Minister shook his head. 'Please. That's too much detail. Just forget Frank. He's a good man. He's on our side – I really believe that.'

'Sir,' Hatty spoke. 'We know you're uneasy about working with children, but we also know what we're doing.'

'I know you do,' the Prime Minister said, 'but it will never stop me feeling uneasy. You're children. It's not right. Not legal. But if you are the only way we can stop the worst things happening, then I know we must. I've got two SAS units half an hour from here in the mountains if we should need them. But I can't use them unless it's absolutely necessary. It would cause an international scandal.'

'You can rely on us, sir.'

'I have no choice,' the Prime Minister confessed. 'But I really do think you're wrong about Frank. Forget him. Tell me, who's your third suspect?'

'An Inuit girl from Canada.'

'A girl? How old?'

'Fourteen maybe?'

'What? A fourteen-year-old Canadian girl? This just gets more absurd. Maybe I should speak to Julia about this. I'm becoming less happy about what you and your friends are doing.'

'It's a small matter at the moment, sir,' Hatty went on. 'She was around when the attack happened this morning. She was filming it. And now the footage is all over YouTube. We suspect she is an activist of some sort. Someone to keep an eye on.'

'Right,' the Prime Minister said, glancing at his watch. 'Look, I'm not happy about any of this, Frank especially. But I have to be at my next meeting. I'm already dreadfully late. Tell me, what are your plans right now?'

'To track all three,' Hatty said. 'Focusing on Esenin and Hawk. We have bugs in some of their clothes and in their rooms, so we're managing to listen in to some of their conversations.'

'OK.' The Prime Minister paused. 'If it were me, I'd focus on the Russian. They have a history of making trouble. They've already tried underhand things to get their hands on the oil and gas up there. By all means, keep an eye on the Americans, but I'm convinced Hawk is clean.'

'We'll keep you informed,' Hatty replied. She knew now wasn't the time to try and convince the Prime Minister that Hawk was a potential suspect. There were more urgent matters at hand. 'Er . . . sir?'

'Yes?'

'Please . . . would you mind giving me a leg-up?'

ON THE EDGE

As Lesh switched the lift back on, using his SpyPad from his room so that the Prime Minister could go on his way, he noticed a movement in one of the monitors on his split screen. Hawk was leaving the hotel.

'Kester. Lily. Go,' Lesh ordered. 'Hawk's on the move.'

Lily and Kester were on their feet immediately.

'Take your coats,' Lesh went on, now watching the American through hotel CCTV corridor cameras he'd tapped into. 'The temperature outside's dropping fast. He's putting his coat on and heading into town. I think he's with another member of the American party. Not sure. You need to find out.'

Lesh was right about the weather. When Kester and Lily got outside, there was an icy breeze coming from the north, dark clouds drifting over the mountains and fjords. But there was no sign of the Americans.

'Where are they?' Lily spoke into the microphone concealed in her watch. 'Is the tracking device still in Hawk's hat?'

'Yes,' Lesh's voice came back to them. 'They're walking to the north of Tromsø town centre. They're just crossing the Bruvegen Bridge. Back towards Tromsdalen.'

Lily and Kester skirted the harbour area and jogged towards the bridge, past small wooden houses painted bright colours, as Lesh satellite-tracked them and Frank Hawk.

When the children reached the western end of the bridge, they could see Hawk and the other American. The two men were already halfway across.

'Where are they going?' Kester asked Lily as they pretended to check a map on a display board.

'Don't know. Maybe just for a walk, but I doubt it. We have no idea, but we can't lose them.'

Crossing the bridge was different from earlier in the afternoon. It felt more like a narrow ribbon of metal stretched over a vast expanse of rough sea-water than a bridge. The sun had gone in behind the clouds and a heavy mist was advancing over the water. The entire north end of the island of Tromsø was already invisible.

They moved on quickly for fear of losing the Americans, jogging, fighting against a wild wind that made speaking – and talking into their mics –

impossible. At the eastern end of the bridge there was no sign of their targets.

Because he knew Kester and Lily had stopped moving, Lesh spoke over the radio. 'Don't stop. Head east, five hundred metres, then south. Can you see the cable car?'

'I saw it before,' Kester shouted above the noise of some trucks.

'They're heading that way,' Lesh confirmed.

The cable car was a large metal box, about the same shape and size as a third of a single-decker bus. It was there to transport tourists to the top of the mountain, so they could admire the view. When Lily and Kester reached the ticket office at the bottom, they could see the cable car suspended on a thick wire, a hundred metres above them, moving slowly towards a wooden building at the top of the steep mountain. A second cable car was coming in the opposite direction down towards them.

'They're in the one going up,' Kester said, keeping himself out of view of the ascending car, like Lily.

'Great. We'll go in this next one,' Lily said.

Once the second cable car had arrived, they paid at a kiosk at the foot of the cable car and climbed aboard, pleased to have it to themselves. The two children gaped in awe at the scenery about them. At first, they looked at the rooftops of the houses around the cable car entrance, then at the rough path beneath. But, within just a minute, they seemed to have travelled miles and were suspended high over Tromsdalen. They could see to the other side of the water above the mist. The panorama was amazing as the weather cleared a little. The massive row of black mountains in the distance. The glint of a plane taking off from the airport on the far side of the island. Tiny boats in the fjords to the south.

'So what's the plan?' Lesh asked over the radio as the cable car approached the summit of the mountain.

'Where are they?' Kester asked.

'Look at a set of benches on a wooden walkway that sticks out off the side of the mountain. Can you see it?'

'Yes,' Lily said. 'There. They're looking across the fjord. Quite near a large group of tourists.'

'Good,' Lesh said. 'If you can get near to them, listen in. Try and stick close. I suspect they've gone up there to have a private conversation where they can be sure there are no bugs.'

Lily identified two ways that she could get close to the Americans to listen in on them.

One option was to walk out of the door of the building where the cable car had dropped them, across the wooden walkway, among the group of thirty or so tourists milling around, but possibly in full view of the men.

The other option was to skirt round the back of the building, climb over a fence that had been put up to stop people falling hundreds of metres down the mountainside, then move sideways along a rough surface until she was *underneath* the wooden walkway, below the men's feet. And to try her best not to fall to her death.

There was really only one viable option, so Lily found herself, feet wedged into a narrow crevice, hands clutching on to icy stone, beneath the wooden walkway. It took her four minutes to get into position.

Lily looked upwards. Through the gaps between the wood, she could see the hiking boots of both men. One had a lace untied which was dangling between the slats. Lily could have easily reached out and pulled it.

'Are we safe here?' Hawk asked the other man, after a few seconds of small talk about the scenery. 'I mean, can anyone overhear us?'

'We're safe here, sir.'

'Good. Good. The device then?'

'Yes.'

'When do we think the Russians are bringing it in?'

'It could be tonight. Maybe in that ship there. Any ship.'

Lily looked down. A ship was already docking on the Tromsdalen side of the water. In the spot where the Russian had been standing the night before.

'Is it viable?' Hawk asked. 'I mean, can it work after all these years?'

'It's viable, sir. I've done some research. It could blow this whole town sky-high and start a world war, no question.'

Lily couldn't believe what she was hearing. If this was true, then they'd stumbled on something just as serious as the PM was expecting.

'So how do we stop them? It would be a mistake to just say the Russians are planning this. No one would believe us. I just wish there were spies here. Anyone. But they're all banned from the conference. For good reason.'

'Sir, I think I know a place where the device may be stored. Before the attack. I have some intelligence. Our people have been monitoring the area with satellites.'

'Where?'

'I'll take you there, sir.'

Hawk said, 'Let's go then.'

Lily had to blink to protect her eyes from the dirt and stones that tumbled through the gaps in the wood as the two men walked away. She started to make a move to get back to Kester so they could trail the Americans.

Then she slipped.

Felt herself falling.

And – for a second – she thought, *This is it. A long fall. A quick death.*

But the fall lasted no longer than a second and, without really hurting herself, Lily found herself at the top of the path that wound directly underneath the cable car. She'd fallen five metres at most. And the ground was soft. Mercifully.

'Are you OK?' Lesh asked anxiously over the radio, having heard her fall.

'Fine,' Lily breathed out.

Next she heard Kester's voice. 'They're in the cable car. Going down. I couldn't get in with them. They'd know I was following them.'

'But they're heading to where they think the Russian device may be,' Lily muttered to herself, eyeing the cable car. 'That's what they said.' Then Lily spoke into her mic. 'Lesh, can you track them when they reach the bottom?'

'I can, but are you sure they're on the move?' Lesh queried. 'I have them at the top on the walkway.'

'Negative,' Kester replied. 'They're in the cable car.'

'And it's moving now,' Lily added, seeing it sliding down its wires.

Lily heard Kester running above her on the walkway. Then she heard him stop. 'He's left his hat,' Kester said.

'We've lost them then.' Lesh's voice. 'Unless one of you can get down to the bottom. Quickly.'

Lily looked out across the islands and mountains

and water, then at the path running steeply down several hundred metres.

'No chance of that,' Kester muttered.

Lesh swore into the microphone. 'We've lost them,' he said. 'It's impossible.'

But Lily shook her head. There had to be a way to do this.

DOWNHILL

Lily knew that the only way she was going to keep up with the cable car's fast descent was by taking risks. If she didn't take those risks, then they'd lose Hawk and his sidekick and miss out on finding out about the dangerous device the two were discussing.

It was about a mile down the hill. A fifty per cent slope. Seriously steep. And that wasn't the only problem. Lily had to run fast. Fast enough to keep herself under the cable car. If she fell too far behind, she'd be visible to them from above.

She had to get this right.

Lily practically threw herself downwards, her right foot hitting the rough track with only a half second for her to think about where to put her left. She had to avoid the larger stones, keep to the solid ground without for a moment slowing down. But Lily had run like this before. In the hills where she used to live. Her dad's passion had been fell-running, taking on the steepest, wildest hills, up and down. And it was a passion he'd passed on to his daughter.

Lily was doing well. She could hear the rattle of the cable car above her. Clanking. Squealing. Grinding. She could even see its shadow moving steadily alongside her. Down she went, her knees jarring. One wrong foot and she could rip her knee or hip out of its socket. All the more likely because she'd not warmed up properly. As she ran, she tried to piece something together in her mind. A worry. The idea that something about what they'd just overheard wasn't quite right. That it sounded like . . . a bit like what Hawk wanted them to hear. But she was running too hard and too fast to think clearly, so she put the thought to the back of her mind. For now.

After two minutes, she was halfway down. Underneath the cable car. That was when she saw the man, an old man, coming slowly up the hill, stooping to admire a flower, then straightening up as he heard her coming. He was on a raised piece of ground. If he was to stand and put his hands in the air, he'd almost be able to touch the cable car that was about to pass over him.

Lily could see no way of avoiding the old man, because of her speed and the steepness of the hill and the bushes on either side. They were locked into a collision course. A collision course that could easily send them both falling hundreds of metres down the mountainside. But it was too late to worry about that. Lily had to keep on Hawk's tail. The mission depended on it.

What happened next took mere seconds. First, Lily heard the clatter of the cable car above her, suddenly louder in her mind. Then, as she hit the hillside with her right foot, she saw the man begin to flinch and duck. One step before they collided.

Lily's left foot came down, then, springing upwards, she was flying over the man, a giant leap, her hands reaching upwards, miraculously gripping the metal tubing on the underside of the cable car.

It was the only way.

Lily's arms were already feeling the strain when she looked down for the best place to drop back down on to the hillside. But she was horrified to see there was absolutely no chance of that. Because she was now suspended over fifty metres above the ground, her legs dangling helplessly as the cable car juddered and swung, the strength draining from her arms already as the wind picked up to rock the cable car from side to side.

How long? she asked herself. *How long can I hang here?* She knew that her legs were strong – from the running – but her arms? She was less sure about them. But Lily knew what she had to do. They had been trained for this. Making the mind take control of the body. She closed her eyes and breathed in and out, keeping her hands gripped on the icy metal tube. She counted to sixty, able to hear the voices of those travelling inside the cable car. One minute. And, when the minute was up, she felt the cable car start to slow. It was going to be OK. She must be nearing the bottom. So Lily opened her eyes.

And it was true that the cable car was slowing. But not to stop at the bottom. It was stopping in mid-air.

With a jolt.

A jolt so sudden that it dislodged one of Lily's hands.

Now she was hanging by one arm.

Lily felt sick and weak, but she tried not to think about her fingers straining to hold on. She looked down. Forty metres at least. She'd never survive a fall like that. She felt her hand slip. A slow, agonizing movement.

This was it.

Lily looked up at the mountain behind her. She thought of how, after the terror of the fall and the pain of hitting the ground, she would inevitably be dead. She tried to think beyond that. How her ghost – if there were ghosts – would be able to run in these mountains with her dad.

Then she heard the voice. 'Hang in there, Lily.'

At first, she thought it was her dad's voice and that she might already be falling. Was this some sort of out-of-body experience?

'Hang in there.' The voice again. And Lily understood that it was not her dad speaking to her from beyond the grave, but Lesh speaking through their comms system.

'Don't fall,' he said. 'It's not worth it. I should know.'

Lily felt her hand grip tighter than ever on the underside of the cable car. She knew Lesh would have been able to tap into the CCTV and would be watching her, reliving his own accident, as horrifying for him, perhaps, as it was for her.

She would do this for him.

The cable car started moving again. Closer to the end of its run. Closer to the ground where she could drop down.

She could feel every individual muscle in her arms tearing and burning, the joints of her fingers ripping apart. If she could just hold on. Then her grip went. Fingers slipping. She looked down.

Twenty metres.

Hold on.

Fifteen metres.

Hold on. But she couldn't. She felt her hand giving way, gravity pulling her downwards.

Ten metres.

Then she dropped. That helpless falling feeling. Then hitting the ground hard.

But not too hard. A drop of maybe five metres. The cable car had reached lower ground. She was OK.

Lily stayed in that position for a minute, stretching her arms, breathing, calming her mind. She whispered into her mic. 'Thanks, Lesh.'

Now to work. In the car park, a bus was waiting. Lily guessed that it was there for the large group of sightseers who had come down the hill. The coach had the word HURTIGRUTEN TOURS on a piece of card at the front, confirming her theory.

Lily squatted behind it, her knees like jelly. And there, alongside the coach, she saw Hawk, standing talking. He was playing them. Somehow he was leading them on. She knew it. And she needed to speak to Kester about it. Now.

Lily glanced up the hill. The second cable car was coming down now. She spoke quietly into her mic.

'Kester? Are you in the cable car?'

She heard Kester reply with a single cough. That meant 'yes'. It also meant he wasn't alone in the car. Lily could hear a hubbub of voices in the background. Kester must be in the cable car with some of the tourists.

'I made it,' she reported, knowing Kester would be unable to talk safely. 'Hawk is here, just chatting to a bus driver. I'm behind the coach. Can you hear me?'

Another cough.

'I'll wait here until they make a move – or until you get here.'

A third cough.

Lily then turned her attention to the Americans. Listening in now she was close enough to overhear. First, she heard Hawk address the driver of the

95

tourist bus. 'Hello there. Can I ask: are you heading back to the boat?'

'Yes. The Hurtigruten,' the driver said with a strong Norwegian accent.

'Can we hitch a lift?' Hawk asked. 'We're keen to take a trip up north, to see a couple of places. On the ship.'

Hawk passed something into the driver's hand. Money.

'No problem,' the driver smiled.

Lily watched the two Americans climb aboard as more tourists flooded out of the cable car, heading for the coach.

'Quickly, please,' the driver called out to the tourists as Lily moved around the bus to see if she could spot Kester.

And there he was, moving with the group, hidden among them as they began a faster walk to board the bus.

'Quickly,' the driver shouted. 'Your boat leaves in thirty minutes. They will not wait for us. We must leave.'

As he spoke, the Hurtigruten boat sounded its horn, the noise echoing harshly off the mountains and escaping up the fjord, and the tourists hurried on to the bus.

Kester ran up beside Lily. 'What's going on?' he asked.

'Hawk's on the bus. He's going to get the boat

north. We have to be on that boat. Then we need to talk. I'm not sure about Hawk. I'm not sure about any of this. But if we don't get on this bus, then the boat, we've no chance of sorting this out.'

'But how do we get on it without being seen?' Kester asked.

BY THE SEA

The sun was dipping behind the mountains to the west of Tromsø, a soft orange light coming off the water. But the city seemed busier than ever, couples walking along the harbourside, groups of children about the same age as the Squad sitting on the grass round rucksacks, laughing, texting, staring at the water. The weather had turned again. It was mild and clear, the cold winds holding off for now.

The large red-and-white Hurtigruten ship that had been dwarfing the harbour was now moving out under the bridge that spanned the fjord. Lesh, Hatty and Adnan sat in a cafe on the edge of the water, three Cokes in front of them. Blending in.

Hatty was gazing out at the fjord, smiling as if she thought it was the most beautiful thing she'd ever seen. In fact, she had her eyes on the ship, watching for Lily and Kester, who had radioed to say they were going onboard after Hawk, having stowed away in the luggage area of a bus, before boarding the ship as foot passengers.

Adnan appeared to be playing a video game, twitching and flicking his finger across a SpyPad, which looked like a perfectly normal iPad. But actually he had hacked into Norway's fjord sonar to scan the dozens of nearby fjords for unusual activity. And Lesh seemed to be checking his texts. In reality, he was looking up Sergei Esenin, the Russian. Desperately trying to find out more about their number-one suspect.

'Nothing,' Adnan said under his breath.

'Hang on,' said Lesh, adjusting his wheelchair so the light coming off the water didn't cause a glare on his SpyPhone screen.

'What?' Hatty asked.

'Esenin. He's . . .'

'Go silent,' Adnan snapped, knowing the others would understand that there was a threat and that they shouldn't talk about the mission.

'What?'

'Hi, Rio! Over here!' Adnan shouted as much to warn the others that Rio and some of the others were approaching.

Hatty and Lesh looked up to see what Adnan had already spotted: Rio, Georgia and Finn walking towards them from the direction of their hotel.

'Hi,' Rio said. 'What are you up to?'

'Nothing much. Just chilling before training later on,' Adnan said. 'You?'

'Same as you. Looking around,' Rio replied. 'We got bored in the hotel.'

Georgia glanced at Lesh's SpyPhone screen and screwed up her face. 'What are you looking at?' Suddenly everyone else was looking at the screen too.

'Baseball?' Rio shouted. 'Why are you reading about baseball?'

Lesh shrugged. 'I like it.'

'I never knew,' Rio went on. 'It's a bit of an *American* sport, isn't it?'

'I like American sport,' Lesh lied.

'Have you been up in the cable car?' Hatty asked, pointing across the water at the tiny metal box that was descending the wooded slope, trying to deflect attention away from Lesh.

'No, have you?' Rio asked, looking half-interested.

'Yes. It's fab. Really wild and windy and the views are great.'

'Urghh,' Georgia said. 'That's the last place I'd want to be in the world.' Then she smiled. 'Now I see why your hair always looks so . . . you know, Hatty.'

Hatty smiled back. 'A least my hair is *my* hair. A natural blonde, are you, Georgia?'

Georgia said nothing.

As the conversation went on, Lesh continued to read his SpyPhone and Hatty could tell that what he was reading was not good news, maybe something that required them to act and act soon. She needed to get rid of Rio, Georgia and Finn.

'The cable car goes on all night,' Hatty said, her attention back on Rio. 'Apparently, if you go up around this time, you can see the Northern Lights sometimes.'

'Really?' Finn was the one who sounded excited now.

'Honestly,' Hatty said. 'And it's a clear night. There's a cafe up there. You can sit and have a drink. Eat. It's supposed to be great.'

'Come on.' Finn, who was normally so quiet, was hopping about from one foot to another like a child asking his mum and dad if he could go.

'OK,' Rio said, then he looked directly at Hatty. 'Are you coming?'

Hatty smiled. She quite liked Rio, but she had other things to do right now.

'We'd better stay with Lesh,' she said, knowing that Rio wouldn't question anything to do with Lesh and his wheelchair.

When the other three had gone, Hatty looked across at Lesh.

'I'm so sorry,' she said. 'I used you as an excuse not to go.'

Lesh grinned. 'Use me all you like. We needed to get shot of them. Anyway, there are more important things to worry about. Lily and Kester – have we heard from them?'

'Not since they radioed from the coach, saying

they were boarding the boat. And Lily said she was starting to suspect Hawk may be playing us. Even Esenin too. That we should bear that in mind.'

'OK. We keep our options open. I just hope they made it onboard,' Lesh muttered. 'Anyway, there's nothing we can do about that right now, so I might as well tell you about this.'

Hatty and Adnan gave Lesh their full attention.

'I've got some more info on Esenin,' Lesh said. 'He works in the oil and gas business and he has a good history of working with other countries. Most Russians have wanted to work alone to get at oil in their part of the Arctic, but Esenin appears to want to cooperate with countries like Norway.'

'So that's good, right?' Adnan asked.

'It is. But there's a bad bit.'

'Which is?' Hatty pushed.

'His dad was an explorer as well as a spy. And he took the young Esenin on a field trip to Greenland when he was a teenager.'

'And?'

'Well, Russians weren't allowed to leave their country very much in those days. Only if the government gave them permission.'

'So?'

'So whatever they were doing must have been fine by the leaders of their country. Normally, whatever was fine by the Russian leaders was pretty dangerous for the rest of the world at that time.

The location they went to was the very same spot where the Americans lost a nuclear warhead in the sixties.'

'Ahh,' said Adnan.

'Oh,' said Hatty.

'And,' Lesh continued, 'Esenin and his dad, according to this, were rescued from Greenland by a Russian submarine. I've checked and it's one that was quite capable of carrying such a warhead.'

The three children stayed silent as an older couple settled down at the table right next to theirs, already studying the menu. When the couple were focused on ordering their meal from the waiter, Lesh leaned into the others.

'So that leaves us to focus on Esenin?' Hatty asked.

Lesh and Adnan eyed Hatty and nodded. They were ready to go, ready to find out whether Esenin did have the warhead and, if he did, where it was and what he was planning to do with it.

TO THE TOP OF THE WORLD

The huge ship moved out of Tromsø harbour and – gradually speeding up – passed under the bridge that spanned the water between Tromsø and Tromsdalen.

Lily and Kester had made it to the boat just in time, hot on the heels of the two Americans who had gone aboard with the other members of the coach party. A huge red-and-white vessel with HURTIGRUTEN written on the side.

Kester gazed up at the ship and calculated that it had at least five storeys. It was larger than most of the buildings in Tromsø. He was amazed such a massive thing could float on water. But he felt the same when aeroplanes took off and he'd been in enough of them to know that they did.

Onboard, they bought tickets at a large wooden desk. Tickets that would take them to a town called Hammerfest. They'd checked the last entry on the computer. It was Frank Hawk. A Tromsø to Hammerfest return. They saw his name on the screen, but not what room he was in.

The journey would take about twelve hours; enough time to find the Americans and gather more intelligence, then reach the most northern town in the world. Here the European land mass stopped and all that was north of it was sea and ice up to the North Pole.

Kester and Lily had rented a cabin with a view out across the water. A bunk bed, a tiny bathroom and barely any floor space. Kester stared out of the porthole that showed the sea speeding past.

'So now what?' Lily asked.

'We search the ship,' Kester said. 'Find the Americans. Listen in on them. Go through their room if we can. Find out where they're going.'

'Come on then,' Lily said, standing up.

'Not yet,' said Kester. 'I read a sign that said everyone goes to eat dinner at seven p.m. It's ten to now. If we wait until everyone's eating, we'll avoid bumping into Hawk by accident. We don't want him to know that we're aboard. It's best to keep a low profile until then.'

As they waited, the pair secured their room, leaving a small camera and microphone device pinned to the wall to monitor any uninvited visitors.

The *Nordlys* was one of fourteen Hurtigruten ships that constantly cruise up and down Norway, serving towns and villages that, in winter, cling to the edge of the ice and rock and are battered by the sea.

Onboard there were three accommodation floors,

narrow corridors running the length of the ship to a large staircase at the bow and stern. Above the accommodation were two more floors of restaurants and cafes. There was even a cinema and a library. It was like a massive floating hotel, stuffed with tourists.

At ten past seven Lily and Kester emerged on to the main cafe floor to hear gentle music playing and a hubbub of voices chattering. Every passenger seemed to be in the dining room for the seven o'clock sitting.

The best place to observe the passengers was from outside, looking in, so Kester led Lily on to the deck. Here a few passengers stood alone, their hands on the rail that stopped them falling into the cold, dark sea below.

For the next fifteen minutes, scarves concealing their faces, Lily and Kester peered from all points into the dining rooms and cafes, Lily working clockwise, Kester anticlockwise. They met at the bow of the ship, a cold breeze rushing towards them from the north.

'Anything?' Kester asked.

'Nothing.'

Kester shook his head. 'They must be in their rooms. I asked if you could get food delivered to your cabin and you can.'

'Or they're not onboard,' Lily suggested. 'And they've tricked us on to this boat to get us away from Tromsø. Just like we said.'

'True,' Kester said.

'When do we stop first?'

'I'm not sure.'

'Let's ask,' Lily said, 'at the main desk. At least then we'll know how much time we have to find him before we decide to get off.'

'OK.'

Kester and Lily walked back into the warmth of the cafes and restaurants, the smell of food and coffee, the noise of laughter, and somewhere, on a higher floor, someone singing.

'Hello.'

Kester and Lily had approached the ship's main reception desk to find a member of the crew manning it alone. The desk was solid, made of light wood and chrome tubing. The crew member was young, wearing her long blonde hair in a ponytail.

'Good evening,' the woman said with a friendly smile.

Lily smiled back and spoke to her as Kester leaned over the counter and glanced at all the paperwork that the woman had been working on.

'Please can you tell me when we stop next?' Lily asked.

'Yes,' the woman said in perfect English, although she was clearly Norwegian. She turned round to study a timetable. 'We stop in three hours. At a town called Skjervøy. Then, after that, at Øskfjord, then Hammerfest.'

While the crew member's back was turned, Lily leaned over and slipped one of her two passports underneath a pile of papers on the desk, then quickly pulled her hand away before the woman turned back round. It was an impulsive act, but a plan had come to her mind and, not consulting Kester, she'd acted without hesitation.

Now the woman was looking at her again, smiling. Lily smiled back and said thank you, then headed up the stairs to the cafe. Kester followed right behind her.

'What did you do just then?'

'I put my false passport in her pile of papers.'

'Why?'

'Because we need to go back and find out what room Hawk is in. And we need an excuse to be snooping around. So, if I can say I've lost my passport, then it's one reason I could be frantically searching through her paperwork.'

'Good thinking,' Kester said.

'But let's wait until later,' Lily cautioned. 'Early tomorrow morning. Then there's a chance the reception will be unmanned.'

'OK,' Kester said. 'And, if it's not, we can always create a distraction.'

WEDNESDAY

THE SHIP PRISON CELL

It was all quiet on the ship when Lily and Kester emerged again from their cabin. They stood out on the deck to go over their plan. The sky was bright with a cold white light. The mountains seemed to be glowing and, although the sea was dark, it looked like liquid silver on the surface.

'If there's someone on the counter, I'll ask for help using the Internet terminals,' Kester said. 'Then you have a look.'

'OK,' Lily agreed.

'Come on then,' said Kester, thrusting his hands deep into his pockets.

They went back inside the ship and walked confidently up to the reception desk. It was empty, as they'd hoped. Kester looked down a long corridor of bedrooms, then up a stairwell to check for people. 'Clear,' he murmured.

Lily moved to the end of the counter and lifted a small hatch, allowing her to step behind the desk. Seeing the passenger list, she began speed-reading the names. Her and Kester's false names were the last on the list. Then she saw Hawk's name and moved her finger to find his room number.

247.

Result.

Lily grinned. But then her face dropped. Suddenly the door from the office behind her was opening and the woman they'd talked to the night before emerged, tightening her ponytail.

At first, she didn't see Lily, then, turning, they came eye to eye, a deep frown appearing on the woman's face.

'Hi,' Lily said, smiling innocently at the woman who had just caught her going through the passenger records.

'What are you doing behind the counter?' the woman asked, ignoring Lily's friendliness. Her tone was harsh, not like the first time they'd spoken. She was wearing her jacket now. Black with gold lines on the cuffs. A uniform that made her look more official.

'I asked what you are doing?' she said again. 'This is a secure area.'

'I'm sorry,' Lily said, almost sounding like she was crying. 'I think I dropped my passport round here and I wanted to find it before . . . before anyone found out. I was worried I'd be thrown off the boat.'

Kester moved to lean on the reception desk to give Lily his moral support.

The woman eyed Lily sceptically. 'You've lost your passport?'

'I'm sorry. I know this looks really bad,' Lily sniffed. 'I just wondered if one of the crew had found it and left it for me here maybe?'

The woman looked even more closely at Lily. Lily felt herself go hot inside her head, but she knew not to show it by blushing. She breathed in and out, keeping her body calm, even though her mind was far from it.

The woman frowned again, then shuffled through the papers in front of her, almost immediately finding the passport Lily had placed there a few hours earlier.

'Ah,' she said, her tone softer now. 'Yes. It is here. But, please, if you had lost it, we would not have thrown you off the boat. We would have helped you. I am sorry you were alarmed.'

Lily smiled and took the passport and said thank you three times, trying to sound like she was truly relieved to have her passport back.

'I'm sorry,' the woman said, 'that I suspected you. I hope I wasn't unkind to you?'

Lily shook her head and smiled again, but the woman still looked upset. 'Please,' she said, 'perhaps you would like to have a tour of the boat? I can show you the interesting areas.'

'Really?' Lily said excitedly.

'Yes. We can go now. It will make me feel better

about upsetting you. You are the only passengers awake and I am bored. Come, follow me. I am Marie-Ann.'

'I'm Iris,' Lily said, remembering to give the same name as the one on the false passport she'd planted. 'And this is Tom.'

As she followed the woman on their tour of the boat, Lily felt bad. Here was a nice woman who'd been trusting and kind, but Lily had lied to her about losing her passport, about her name and about what she was doing. It was part of her job, she knew. That was what you had to do to be a spy: to stop greater evils, you had to lie.

But she didn't always feel good doing it.

Marie-Ann tapped a keyboard at the side of a doorway, entering a four-digit code which Kester memorized in case it proved useful later. Lily and Kester followed her through a heavy metal door that was painted white, then down a series of long corridors with other corridors leading off them.

First, she showed them the kitchen storage area and a row of room-sized fridges and freezers packed with food. The children were interested to see hundreds of boxes and giant tins of food, then, in the meat freezer, whole animal carcasses hanging on hooks in cold storage. Next Marie-Ann led them through another door and they found themselves out at the stern of the ship, low down near the water, the sea churning in the morning light. Around them they saw huge ropes coiled or stretched out across the deck. Kester worked out that above them, on the next deck, was the place they had stared out to sea late last night.

'I had no idea we were at the stern of the ship,' he said.

'It is a real labyrinth,' Marie-Ann said. 'But follow me. This is the interesting place.'

Their guide led them down another narrow corridor with a low ceiling. *All* the ceilings were low in the crew area: not like where the passengers sat and walked.

'This,' she said. 'What do you think it is?'

It was a small room with a bed and toilet, both bolted to the floor. A tiny porthole. Nothing else. No bedding. No light fittings.

'A sick bay?' Kester suggested as Lily moved inside the room.

'No,' Marie-Ann smiled. 'This is the jail. For prisoners.'

Lily instinctively stepped back out of the cell. 'Who do you put in here?'

'People who steal. People who drink too much and are . . . vi–' The Norwegian fought to pronounce the word correctly.

'Violent?' Kester suggested.

'Yes. Violent. Now, can you hear this?' Kester and Lily listened.

'What?'

Marie-Ann opened a door and led them along another corridor towards a loud cacophony of noise.

'This is the way to the engine room.' Marie-Ann raised her voice above the grinding, hammering racket. She handed them two pairs of small yellow foam plugs, pointing at their heads. 'For your ears.' Then she put a pair in her ears too.

None of them spoke as they walked through a strange landscape of huge metal pipes and dials and rattling pistons, some silver and pumping, some painted yellow and white. It was like an alien landscape, the engine room taking up the same space as a large house, set on three floors. Looking up, they could see a forest of tubes and wires. All the noise and machinery made it hard to think and they were relieved to emerge out of the engine room into another large space filled with screens and computers.

Marie-Ann took her earplugs out. 'This is where the engines are controlled.'

The tour went on and – for the time it took place – Kester forgot he was a spy and that the tour was just a diversion to stop them getting into trouble. He was so amazed by what he was seeing: the insides of a massive ship that most people never got the chance to see.

He followed Marie-Ann and Lily through more corridors and up extremely steep metal stairways.

Kester tried to piece together where they had been and how it related to the rest of the ship, the places the public were allowed to go. This was like a different world, like a parallel universe that you could duck in and out of, corridors running alongside each other, completely hidden from the public, like secret passageways in an old house.

Then another door opened and they found themselves in the public area of the boat again, out of the cold white corridors that the crew had to put up with every day and into the warm, carpeted, comfortable public areas, face to face with the two American men they had been searching for.

Frank Hawk recognized them immediately.

THE AMERICAN

'Hey! It's the English kids from Tromsø. The soccer players, right?'

The American had his arms open, like Kester and Lily were lifelong friends he'd not seen for years. He was wearing a patterned shirt and holding a yellow jumper over his arm.

Lily grinned at him, but said nothing. She would leave the talking to Kester.

'Hello. It's nice to see you again,' Kester said, sounding calm. 'What are you doing onboard? I thought you were involved in the conference.'

Frank Hawk glanced briefly at his colleague, who was also wearing a shirt under a colourful jumper. They were dressed as if they were about to go and play a round of golf.

'Well, we wanted to see something of the area,' Hawk explained. 'And, you know, the next day of the conference is about paperwork, so here we are. We thought we'd take in some views. Are you heading out there too? What brings you aboard? Don't you have a soccer game coming up? Training?'

Kester shook his head. 'Iris wanted to see the Northern Lights,' he said, knowing that Hawk had never heard Lily's real name. 'We were told we had a better chance if we headed further north.'

'It's a dream of mine,' Lily added seamlessly.

'Wonderful.' The American rubbed his hands together. 'For me too. It'd be good to talk to you kids some more. Hear about your lives in England. You know, I'm having dinner with the captain tonight. How about you two join us? We need some kids around to stop the conversation getting too boring. What do you say?'

Lily expected Kester to find a convincing reason to say no. Why would they want to have dinner with a suspect? It was true they needed to observe him, but that would be getting a bit too close.

She was surprised by his answer.

'Yes, please,' Kester said, sounding excited. 'Do you think the captain will mind?'

'He'll love it,' the American replied. 'Who wouldn't?'

'Thank you,' Kester finished. 'That's very kind of you.'

'Why?'

Lily was marching along the length of one of the

ship's corridors, Kester trying to keep up with her. The two Americans had gone the other way to have breakfast.

'What?'

'Why are we having dinner with that man? We have no idea what he's up to.'

'It'll be interesting, Lily. We need to get close to him. To find out more. He knows something about that warhead. That may even be why he's here. This is the perfect way to do that.'

'Hmmm,' Lily said. 'We're going to have to be really careful.'

They stopped when they reached room 247.

'This is his room,' Kester whispered, looking both ways. 'Quickly now.'

Lily nodded and held her SpyPhone up to the door. Immediately, the lock lit up and beeped. Kester pushed the door open and they both disappeared inside, quietly easing the door shut. Without speaking, Lily passed Kester three small pin-sized bugging devices. Two cameras and one microphone. Kester carefully chose the best angles and placed them above the door, in the corner of the bathroom mirror and on the rim of the room's large square window. The room was at least four times as big as theirs. Lots of space. A nice desk and a bar filled with bottles. There was even a sofa.

'It's funny,' Kester said to Lily. 'One minute we're

being all friendly with him, accepting his dinner invitation: the next we're rifling through his room.'

Lily shrugged. It was true. She had that same thought every day.

They lied.

They deceived.

They cheated.

They were spies.

Fifteen seconds after they'd entered the room, ready to leave, Kester glanced out of the window, just to compare the American's view to theirs. He saw early morning light coming off the sea and one of the two enormous lifeboats suspended on the side of the ship.

'Ready?' he asked Lily.

'Ready.'

Time to leave. But, as Lily reached for the door, turned the handle and pulled it open, Kester's mind jumped back.

To the light coming off the water.

To the lifeboat.

'Shut the door,' he whispered.

Lily shut it and watched Kester drop to the red-and-white carpet, roll underneath the square window and stand again, concealed by the dark blue curtain hanging on the other side. She knew not to ask questions. If Kester wanted her to do anything, he'd say so. She understood he'd have a very good reason for doing what he was doing.

Kester slowly moved the edge of the curtain away from the window so that he was concealed from anyone who might be looking in from outside. He looked out and waited. Kester's dad used to take him birdwatching when he was a boy. *When you're watching for something*, his dad had said, *you may not see it straight away. You might have to wait.*

So Kester waited, aware that Lily was watching him, wondering what he was doing, her back to the door of the American's cabin. And he knew that she would be thinking the same as him. What if the American comes back? What are the chances he'll return? It'd happened once before. They'd never get away with it twice.

This part of spying was a bit like a game. A game of chance. It was most likely that the two Americans were still downstairs eating their breakfast and that they'd be there for another ten minutes at least. But there was also a chance they were about to head down the corridor and come into this cabin, catching Lily and Kester, who had absolutely no means of escape.

That was Kester's gamble.

But for Kester these were just minor worries. He concentrated on the very front of the nearest lifeboat. He'd seen a fleck of light coming from there. Just like the ones coming off the sea. But there was nothing on the boat for the light to reflect off. That was what had stopped him. That was what had made him turn back.

Kester was always asking himself questions and this was one he needed an answer for. It was time to take another risk.

'Lily?'

'Yeah?'

'Walk across the room so you can be seen from the window.'

Lily edged round a table and two chairs, moved slowly in front of the window, then back to the door and Kester saw what he was looking for immediately.

The edge of the tarpaulin that covered the lifeboat lifted and two hands emerged, pointing a camera at the window, a flash of light coming off its lens.

'Open the door,' Kester said, crawling towards it to join his friend.

'What is it?'

'Someone was filming us from the lifeboat.'

Lily pulled the door open. 'Come on then,' she said. 'Let's get out there. Now.'

FAMILY

The lifeboat surprised them now that they were standing next to it on the deck. When they'd looked at the row of bright orange lifeboats from the harbourside in Tromsø, the boats had been dwarfed by the massive ship. But up close, this one was very big, capable of carrying at least fifty people. It was held in place by a large iron winch that would allow it – if needed – to be dropped down the side of the ship and into the sea. Its dark canopy was tied down loosely with rope.

Kester and Lily approached it from the back, slow and silent footsteps on the empty deck. Kester squeezed between the rail on the edge of the ship and the lifeboat. There was just enough room for him to edge close to the spot he'd seen the hands and the camera appear. Lily crept up the other side, looking out for other passengers. They closed in, hoping their quarry hadn't seen them coming, wondering who it was they were stalking, knowing it wasn't Hawk who they'd seen inside the ship earlier.

But it had. Suddenly a figure burst out of the front of the lifeboat, leaping on to the main deck, landing to accelerate towards the rear of the ship. But Lily was already closing in before the figure had even hit the deck. She took two long strides, then rugby-tackled it down on to the wet wooden surface of the deck, as one of the figure's shoes spun off.

'OK. OK,' a voice said as Lily twisted the figure on to its back, her fist raised, ready to strike.

A girl's voice. And one Lily knew.

'You!' Lily shouted. 'The Canadian girl!' as Kester came crashing down beside her, to hold the girl's arms. 'The one from the hotel and the match. Katiyana?'

Both Lily and Kester could feel the wet and coldness of the deck seeping into their clothes as they kept the girl pinned down.

'Yes. It's me!' the girl screamed. 'Let me go.'

Lily was furious. But there was no time to give in to the anger. Lily forced her hand over the protesting girl's mouth. Someone was coming. Another passenger. A man in a waterproof jacket with a woolly hat on, walking round the outside of the ship, aiming a camera at the mountains, then the water, not seeing or hearing these three children grappling on the deck.

Lily let the girl go and eyed her aggressively. 'Follow us and don't say a word,' she said. 'Or we'll come after you.'

'I'll come,' the girl said. 'I'll come.'

Before the other passenger reached them, Lily picked up Katiyana's shoe – a fur-lined boot – and handed it to the girl, making sure she was following. Katiyana's hood had come down, revealing her shiny dark hair. Kester walked behind.

'Good morning,' Lily said to the passenger, smiling. But on the inside she was not smiling. Her mind was sparking with questions. Was this girl a threat? Why was she spying on them? Would she try to escape? Would she say something in front of this other person? Did she know about the Squad? Was she involved with the warhead? What would they do with her if the answer to any of those questions was yes?

The girl walked calmly with them, making no attempt to escape. The three children went to the very rear of the ship where you could stand and watch the churning of the massive propeller. It seemed like the propeller, powered by that massive engine room down below, was moving tonnes of water every second.

When Lily stopped, the girl stopped too, her hands out in front of her as if she was trying to show that she was not armed.

'Why were you spying on us?' Lily spat.

'I wasn't.'

Lily grabbed the girl by the collar. 'Yes, you were. Don't lie. You were taking pictures of us.'

'Not of you,' the girl pleaded.

Lily glanced at Kester, who was looking at her with a questioning face. Lily knew what that meant: go easy. She frowned and released the girl. 'Explain,' she said.

The girl breathed in, then spoke. 'I was watching Frank Hawk. You were in his room. I was hoping to take pictures of *him*. Not you.'

'Why?' Lily pressed, suddenly a lot more interested in what Katiyana was trying to tell her.

'I've told your friends why. And I'm sure they've told you. He's killing the planet.'

'They told me.' Lily narrowed her eyes.' But is that all it is? What's your backstory?'

'I'm from northern Canada,' the girl gasped. 'My family are Inuit. We live in the extreme north in a place called Nunavut. But his search for oil and gas is destroying our lands.'

Lily stepped back ever so slightly. She felt chastened. This girl was telling the truth. She was saying everything that Lily had read about on the plane to Tromsø. That the people who live in the Arctic are in danger, their way of life about to be obliterated. All because of the frantic search for oil and gas and the melting of the ice.

'What do you hope to achieve just by taking photos of him?' Kester cut in, noticing Lily had stalled.

'Anything. If I can find anything about him that makes him look bad, we might be able to break him.'

'Like what?'

'Whatever we can find out about what he likes to do. Anything that will reveal how truly bad he is.'

'But you have no idea of anything he might be doing?'

'Apart from destroying the planet,' Katiyana said. 'But the world seems to think that it's OK, so we're looking for something else, and that's why I'm here. Other members of my organization are in the USA or working undercover in oil and gas fields, trying to find out information.'

'Who sent you? White Fear?' Lily asked.

'They are my family,' Katiyana replied. 'My people.'

Lily leaned against the barriers at the ship's stern that stopped her falling into the sea. Listening to this girl talking about her family, her people and that she did what she did because of them, made Lily envy her. Katiyana had family. Lily longed for her parents at that moment. Her mum. Her dad. The way she used to love them and how they loved her.

'I'm sorry,' Lily said. 'I wasn't sure about you.'

'Please,' Katiyana said. 'You had a right to be unsure. I don't want to know who you are or what you're doing here. But maybe we can help each other. You were in Hawk's room looking for something. Or planting bugs. If you know something, it could help me. I'll tell you everything that I know. Perhaps we can stop him.'

'We're not sure about anything yet,' Kester said.

'Katiyana, I need to speak with Lily. About you. About this. Can we meet later and talk some more? Maybe after the ship goes quiet tonight.'

'Yes,' Katiyana said. 'After everyone's gone to bed?'

'Yes,' Kester agreed. 'We . . .' He glanced at Lily to check he should mention the dinner tonight with the captain and Hawk. Lily nodded.

'We're eating with the ship's captain and Hawk tonight. Hawk invited us. We'll talk to him, press him about Canada. Perhaps there's information that we've both gathered that could help all of us.'

'Yes. That sounds fair. But, please, be careful. Look after yourselves. Frank Hawk is not a good man.'

ORDERS FROM ABOVE

Back in Tromsø – and back in front of the Prime Minister – the children had no time to feel nervous. Even without Kester being there, they had a job to do and were determined to do it. Here they were, reporting to the most powerful man in the UK, giving him information that might help him make some of the most serious decisions that a person had to make.

This time Adnan and Hatty, standing by Lesh's side, had not come in via the roof. They'd come in a staff lift, one used to deliver room-service food.

The Prime Minister stared hard at Lesh as he spoke.

'We have evidence that Sergei Esenin is involved in moving a 1960s nuclear warhead,' Lesh said. 'Evidence both in paperwork and things we've heard the American, Frank Hawk, say when we were bugging him.'

'Go on,' he said in a measured voice. But the children could tell, by the look of thunder on his face, that the mention of Frank Hawk's name again had not impressed him.

Lesh tried not to be distracted by the wind wuthering off the top of the building. He sensed that the weather was changing.

'Esenin was in Greenland in 1992, on an expedition with his father, who was a scientist.'

'Or who may have been pretending to be a scientist,' Hatty interrupted.

'Meaning?' the PM asked.

Lesh explained. 'The evidence could be telling us that they weren't on a scientific mission. It's possible they were there to recover a missing warhead that the Americans lost in 1968.'

'And we also found charts for the channels around Tromsø,' Adnan added. 'One way to look at it is that Esenin is bringing the warhead here. To attack the conference.'

'But that's unconfirmed,' Lesh said, glancing at Adnan and wishing he'd keep his mouth shut. 'We need to find out more to see if there's any truth in that.'

'No, I disagree,' the Prime Minister said, gesturing to Adnan, raising his voice. 'We need to stop him. Now.'

Lesh shook his head before he could stop himself. Hatty noticed the Prime Minister looking almost angrily at Lesh. As if he couldn't believe this boy was telling him what to do.

'I don't think we have enough evidence, sir,' Hatty said to the Prime Minister, backing Lesh up. 'Like Lesh said, there's still a lot of guesswork involved. We could be wrong. I think what we need to do is focus all our attention on Esenin. If we make a mistake, it could be bad news for the conference – and the world.'

'No,' the PM said. 'I've got British Special Forces in the mountains. I can have them come in and do a quiet job. We have too much to lose.'

'With respect, sir,' Hatty said sharply, remembering that this was what adults sometimes said to each other when they were going to say something *without* respect, 'we need more time. There's nothing else to suggest Esenin is behind any real threat to the conference. Bringing in Special Forces would ruin the whole conference and the UK would never be trusted again.'

The room went silent. Even the noise of the wind buffeting off the top of the hotel seemed to stop. The Prime Minister looked at Hatty. It was clear to her that he wasn't used to being spoken to like that. But the thing about Hatty was she didn't care. The most important thing in the world to her was that she should speak her mind, whoever she was talking to, whether it was a five-year-old child or the Prime Minister of the United Kingdom. And, at this point, she wasn't sure what the difference was between the two.

'Twelve hours,' the Prime Minister said. 'That's all you have. Then I call the SAS in.'

'And start a world war?' Hatty muttered under her breath.

'I'm sorry?' the Prime Minister said.

Lesh spoke up. 'Hatty said, "Thank you for giving us more." More time, that is. But we need to go now, sir.' He glanced at his SpyPad. 'Esenin is on the move.'

'That was so cool,' Adnan said in the service lift as the children descended to the ground floor. 'You just cornered the Prime Minister. I wish Lily and Kester had been here to see that.'

'There's no time to worry about them,' Hatty said. 'What are we going to do about Esenin?'

'Follow him. Search his room. Bug him,' Lesh said, glancing at his SpyPhone. 'He left his room while we were with the PM. He's gone with a coat on and a map of the town. He's . . . where is he now? Right now . . . he's walking south towards the Polaria Museum. Sightseeing maybe?'

'Or,' Adnan suggested, 'if you follow the Prime Minister's logic – he's gone to pitch the world into war.'

'Maybe.' Lesh smiled grimly.

'I have to say,' Adnan went on, 'I sort of agree with the Prime Minister. I think Esenin is planning something. I'd have the SAS in here sharpish.'

'You made that clear in there,' Hatty said, gently pushing Adnan against the side of the lift. 'I think you like the Prime Minister.'

'Maybe I do,' Adnan said. 'He's a bit like my dad was.'

Hatty paused as the lift slowed. She couldn't help thinking, as she knew Adnan now was, about his chance of a new family with his uncle from Pakistan. She put her arm round him. 'Your dad was way better than him,' she said.

The lift doors opened and the trio walked quickly through a large kitchen area, finding a door out on to the harbourside, to be hit with a blast of cold air.

'The forecast said that the weather was about to change,' Lesh grumbled as he tightened his scarf and drew his collar round his neck.

'Come on then,' Hatty said. 'Let's move it. We need to follow him, see what he's up to. If we don't, then our glorious leader will have the SAS charging down that hill before we know what's hit us.'

POLARIA

Adnan studied the Polaria Museum building as the three children made their way towards it.

'I hate museums,' Hatty muttered. 'They're boring.'

'I love them,' retorted Adnan.

'You would.'

'What does that mean?'

'It means,' Hatty explained, 'that you're the kind of person who likes boring things, Adnan.'

'Thanks,' Adnan said. 'I like to think of myself as someone who's interested in the big wide world. Someone who wants to know more than he already knows. I wonder if that makes *me* boring – or someone else?'

'Yawn,' Hatty said.

'You're the yawn, Hatty.'

As they reached the door of the museum, Adnan shoulder-barged Hatty. Playfully. Hatty glared back at him. Less playfully.

Polaria was a strange-looking building. It appeared

like a stack of blocks of ice, falling like giant white dominoes, as if they were going to tumble into the fjord. The entrance was a massive sheet of glass, revealing everything inside. A shop. A cafe. The museum itself.

'There's fish,' Adnan said.

'What?' Hatty asked.

'Fish,' Adnan went on. 'In the museum. Fish to look at.'

'I hate fish too,' Hatty said, turning to see that Lesh had stopped his wheelchair and was eyeing the museum warily.

'What's up?' Adnan said. 'Do you hate fish too?'

'Be serious, Adnan,' Lesh snapped. 'There's something in there that Hatty hates even more than fish and museums,' he explained.

'Eh?' Adnan looked blankly at him.

'In there.'

'What?' Hatty joked. 'Georgia?'

Then, to her horror, she saw that Lesh was nodding. And smirking. 'She's in the shop.'

Hatty put her hand to her head. 'Oh no. I have to go in a *fish museum* that has *Georgia* in it. This could not get any worse.'

After paying their entrance fee – and before they were allowed into the main museum – they were directed into a cinema to watch a short film about the Arctic. Ignoring the film, they made their way through a set of tanks filled with fish and seals, then past some interpretation boards and a model of a fishing boat, quickly closing in on the cafe.

'Any sign of Georgia?' Hatty asked.

'Negative,' Lesh said. 'She's not in the shop. It looks like she's gone.'

'Is Esenin still here, more importantly?'

'Yes. In the cafe, by the look of it.'

'Let's go up there then. See what he's doing. OK?'

'OK.'

There was a set of stairs to the left that led up to the cafe, which was over the museum shop. And a lift. The children bundled into it and started to ascend. When the lift door opened and they saw the cafe and everyone in it, none of the three said a word, although each was reeling in shock at what met their eyes. There were about ten people in there, most sitting drinking coffee. Some were eating. At the table in the far corner, overlooking the car park, was Sergei Esenin.

He was sitting – and talking – to another person.

Georgia.

GEORGIA

Hatty, Lesh and Adnan sat at the table nearest the lift.

'Act normal,' Hatty said. 'Adnan, get some drinks and cakes or something.'

Adnan stood up and walked towards the counter and the array of cakes and open sandwiches displayed in a glass case.

Hatty observed Georgia. The blonde girl followed Adnan with her eyes, like she was looking at a stranger, then she returned her attention to the Russian, without even acknowledging Hatty.

'She knows we're here,' Hatty whispered to Lesh.
'She does.'
'So what's she doing?'
'No idea.'
'I do,' Hatty spat. 'She knows about us. You know? What we do! She must do.'

'No way,' Lesh said, angling the SpyPad so that he could film the pair as evidence.

'She does. Or she thinks we're up to something.

But why's she talking to him? How could she possibly know him? She has no idea of the danger she's in. This could completely wreck our mission. She could easily end up dead.'

Hatty watched the pair closely. Georgia was wearing clothes and make-up that made her look at least eighteen.

When Adnan came back with three cans of Coke and some biscuits, Hatty drew him close.

'What did you see?' she asked.

'A man who likes the attention,' Adnan said. 'He loves that she's listening to him talk.'

'Urghhh!' Hatty grimaced.

'So what do we do?' Adnan asked.

'We wait,' Hatty said, looking at Lesh for approval. He nodded.

After fifteen minutes of waiting, Hatty was still fuming. She was desperate to get her hands on the other girl. She wanted to throttle her. Georgia was about to blow their mission by meddling with their key target. But then Georgia stood up and smiled at the man, pointing back down the stairs.

'She's going to the toilet,' Hatty muttered. 'I'll go after her.'

Hatty watched as the Russian stood politely, then sat down smiling after Georgia had gone. She counted to twenty, then followed the other girl down the staircase, across the museum floor and into the Ladies. As she left, Lesh grabbed her arm.

'What?'

'Go easy,' Lesh said. 'This is sensitive. Don't let how you feel about Georgia get in the way of what we need to achieve here.'

Hatty pulled her arm away, then breathed out, her eyes closed. When she opened them, she touched Lesh on the shoulder. 'OK,' she agreed. Then she was off.

All the way down the stairs, Hatty kept telling herself to be calm. Yes, she hated Georgia, but Georgia was involved now. There was no getting away from it. Lesh was right. Hatty couldn't blow this. She pushed open the door of the toilet. It was bright and white inside. She took a deep, calming breath.

'What the hell are you doing?' she shouted.

'What do you mean?' Georgia answered. 'I'm just talking to a guy.'

Hatty checked all the cubicles, keeping her eyes on Georgia, who was standing at the mirror. All the toilets were empty.

'Why?' Hatty asked.

'Why what?'

'Why are you talking to this man?'

'He's nice, interesting.'

'Why *this* man?' Hatty insisted.

'You're asking me why?' Georgia said.

'Yes.'

'Let's look at this another way.' Georgia was

smiling now. 'Why are *you* following him?'

For a few seconds Hatty was speechless. She had absolutely no idea how Georgia knew they were pursuing Esenin. But she knew she had to speak, to act as if that was not what they were doing.

'We're not.'

'You are. Don't lie. I saw you coming here from the hotel, looking around for someone. There's no way you'd be looking for me. I've seen you snooping round the hotel too, like you're private detectives or something. I watch you all the time. You're rubbish at it.' Georgia stopped and faced Hatty without blinking.

Hatty felt like punching Georgia in the mouth at this point. The whole mission was in jeopardy here. No, it was more than that. The entire future of the Squad was at risk. They'd been compromised – by this stupid little princess – and that was the truth of it.

The problem was that Hatty, for once, didn't know what to say. She was genuinely shocked. And that gave Georgia a further chance to fill the silence.

'I said there was something about you lot at the football yesterday,' she said. 'I've been watching you. Ever since the five of you showed up in Poland, I've known that you're more than footballers. You'd have to be because you're rubbish at football. I think you're undercover detectives. Something like that. What is it? Investigating football? And I think

I'm about to find out more, thanks to Sergei up there. And, when I know more, I think I'd like to join you to be honest. I've always liked detective stories.'

Hatty smiled. So Georgia wanted to be a detective? Maybe that was how she could sort out this situation. Could she get away with that? Let the other girl think she was helping them with detective work? For now it felt to Hatty like her only option. There was no other way she could get out of this conversation and try to keep tabs on Esenin, both of which needed doing urgently. So long as she could say they were undercover football detectives, then she wouldn't have to admit that they were spies. Yes, it was true that spies and detectives are a little similar, but Hatty felt it would be a result not to have to admit exactly what they were.

'OK,' Hatty said.

'OK what?'

'You're right.'

'Right about what?'

'We're undercover. We're detectives.'

'Ha! I knew it.'

'I need to be honest about something else,' Hatty said.

'Yeah?' Georgia looked really cocky now, like she was clever and she knew it.

'You know that I put on this act that I don't like you?' Hatty said.

'Yeah?'

'That's not an act. I don't like you.'

'Thanks,' Georgia said, looking slightly wounded.

Hatty hoped she'd not gone too far. Say something to hurt the other girl, then tell her lots of nice things about herself. It was a technique they'd been trained in. A way of making someone join you, rather than be against you.

'But . . .'

Georgia remained silent.

'But, regardless of that, we do need you to join us. We do need your help. You've managed to get to our target where we've failed. And, though it's hard for me to say it, I admire you for that. I underestimated you. Without your help, we can't complete our operation.'

Georgia was smiling now. Broadly. Hatty tried to smile too, but all the time she knew this was a colossal risk. Something that could backfire terribly. A gamble. A terrible gamble.

'Please,' Hatty said, putting her doubts to one side. 'Will you help us?'

Exactly three minutes after Georgia had left the cafe, closely followed by Hatty, the two boys saw Georgia coming back up the stairs. The Russian had his back to her as he tapped his mobile phone.

Georgia took the opportunity to wink at Lesh and Adnan, then she flicked her hair and rejoined the

Russian. Neither boy reacted. They just looked at each other, puzzled. They had expected Hatty to persuade the other girl to leave. *This* was not how they thought the situation would develop. And then Hatty was sitting back down with them, accompanied by the sound of Georgia laughing at the Russian man's latest remark.

'What?' asked Lesh.

Hatty frowned. 'I've recruited Georgia,' she said calmly and quietly. 'She's wired. She's going to ask him about the warhead. I've briefed her about the case. But I've told her that we're detectives, OK? That's the story.'

'Wired?'

'Yes, she's got a pin mic on her top.'

Lesh and Adnan said nothing. But both their jaws were hanging open.

'Are you mad?' Lesh asked eventually. 'She's just a girl. She's not trained. She's not anything.'

'She's clever,' Hatty said grudgingly. 'And, frankly, we had no choice. Come on, Lesh. Adnan, you stay up here. Lesh and I are going to listen in to what she gets him to say.'

QUESTIONS AND ANSWERS

'I love the mountains,' Georgia said.

Her voice was clear through the headphones both Lesh and Hatty were listening through, sitting underneath the cafe next to a model of a fishing boat. Hatty knew what Georgia was up to mentioning mountains. She'd briefed her about extreme walking, exploration, even the warhead. All to see if Georgia could get Esenin to open up about his own experiences.

'Yes. Very beautiful,' the Russian replied.

'My friends and I,' Georgia went on, 'we're planning to walk across them. In the snow. It'll be exciting.'

'No, no,' Esenin warned. 'It is too dangerous. There can be ice. One slip and can be death.'

'You talk like you've had an accident yourself,' Georgia said, sounding scared.

A pause. Hatty held her breath. She wondered if their new recruit had gone too far. She was already pushing the Russian for information about his hiking trip with his father. Not softening him up first. Georgia really wasn't cut out for this. But Hatty was mistaken.

'Yes,' he said. 'This is true.'

'Tell me more.'

Hatty frowned. She could just imagine Georgia now, hanging on to his every word, like he was the most interesting man in the world. The thought appalled her. But she knew it was the right tactic. Georgia was playing him like a true spy.

'When I am young. Your age. My father takes me on an . . . how do you say . . . expedition. To Greenland. Do you know it?'

'Yes. It's near Canada. Was it icy?'

'Yes.' Esenin laughed loudly. 'Icy. Very icy. We walk on ice for days. We carry our items . . . our foods . . . on sledges behind us. Ice, ice, ice.'

'Wow,' Georgia gushed. 'All by yourself?'

'Yes.' Esenin sounded excited now. 'My father says I must carry everything for me. He will not help me. He says it is to make me a man.'

'Well, he was right,' Georgia said, making Hatty wince. 'Did the trip go well?'

'Very well. My father . . .' The Russian faltered. 'I don't know if to tell you. It is not good.'

Hatty pricked up her ears. Could this be what they were after? She swallowed and began to think that recruiting Georgia had been a good idea. A risk, yes, but it was looking like it might pay off.

'Please tell me,' Georgia said.

'No. This is a bad thing. I am not proud of this. It is a thing from the past. Not something for now.'

'Please. You can't shock me.'

Hatty could hear a slight edge of fear in the man's voice. Like he was not sure he was comfortable talking about what Georgia was asking, but, at the same time, he wanted to tell her, impress her.

'OK,' Esenin said. 'My father . . . he . . . he shoots a polar bear.'

'How exciting,' Georgia said.

Hatty hoped Georgia was acting. What could be exciting about shooting an amazing animal like a polar bear?

'But then the weather changes and it becomes dangerous. It is as if the killing of the bear is a bad thing against nature. The storm comes. We hoped to head north. But we are driven back. We are rescued in the end. By a Russian boat.'

'Oh, how frightening,' Georgia said. 'Did you bring anything back with you? Any souvenirs? Or did you leave with nothing?'

'Souvenirs?'

'Yes. Like things you found there. Things that remind you of your trip.'

'No. I wish it. But no. Just Father and me. We leave our clothes and food. Only take away what we are wearing. But I do bring one thing. When the polar bear dies and the storm begins, I begin to think that we did the wrong thing, that we disrespected nature. That the storm was a warning to us. Since then I have carried this with me in my heart. I wanted the bear's dying to mean something. That my life must be for saving the world, not destroying it.'

Hatty looked at Lesh and frowned. Georgia had done well. She had tried to find out if Esenin had been involved with retrieving the warhead, but he'd not admitted to anything. And he'd seemed completely natural, as if he was innocent and not about to tip the world into a third world war.

'Do you think she'll stop now?' Lesh asked. Hatty was about to reply, but then they heard Georgia's voice again.

'I read somewhere that there was an American warhead hidden or lost in Greenland. Did you see that?'

Hatty gasped. So direct. Georgia was taking the biggest risk of all. Hatty had only told her about that as background, not as something to say.

This was now officially a disaster.

DEBRIEF

Hatty, Adnan and Lesh kept Georgia in the cafe of Polaria for an hour after Esenin had gone. They wanted to debrief her after her conversation with the Russian, discover all the other things she had found out. The non-verbal things.

Had Esenin looked nervous about what he was telling her at any point?

Did she think at any moment that the Russian was lying?

As they spoke, Adnan struggled to hide his admiration for Georgia. 'You were great,' he said.

'Thank you,' Georgia said, tightening her hair into a ponytail.

'No, really. You were cool and calm and you asked all the right questions. It was brilliant.'

'Thanks, Adnan.'

Hatty squirmed in her seat as she watched Adnan fawning over Georgia. But she kept quiet.

'The best bit was when you asked him about his dad and the missing warhead,' Adnan went on. 'And he said his dad would have made him carry the bomb through an ice storm if he'd have known it was there.'

'How did he seem when you asked him about the warhead?' Lesh broke in, wanting to get back to the facts.

'Surprised,' Georgia replied.

'Properly surprised?'

'I'd say so, yes. I don't think he was lying. He looked me in the eyes, then he seemed to laugh.'

'How about when he was laughing about it. Did that seem genuine?'

'Very.'

'You mustn't mention this to anyone else,' Hatty emphasized.

'I won't,' she said. 'But since I took a risk for you, will you take one for me and tell me who you're working for? This isn't what I expected detectives to be looking into.'

'Georgia,' Hatty interrupted. 'You've done us a great favour. Really. Yes, we're detectives, like you worked out. But we can't tell you anything more.'

Hatty kept her eyes on Georgia, a hard, unwavering gaze. It seemed to do the trick.

'OK,' Georgia replied, frowning. 'I understand. But can I ask one more thing?'

'Go on,' said Hatty.

'This isn't all a game, is it? I mean, this is real. I can tell it's real. It's to do with the attack on the hotel yesterday, isn't it? And why Lily and Kester have disappeared. They're involved, right?'

'That's all we can say,' Hatty replied firmly. Georgia nodded. The others could tell she understood.

'I wish I could help,' she said.

'We need to go to training,' Lesh said, glancing anxiously at his watch. 'You can help us by making sure none of the other players ask too many questions.'

LIES

Hatty, Adnan, Lesh and Georgia rushed into the centre of Tromsø to find a single car at the city's main taxi rank. It was a full-sized cab, meaning Lesh could ride in his wheelchair. Hatty and Adnan helped him aboard.

The taxi driver was a tall man, his legs so long that his knees touched the steering wheel. The taxi had two car stickers on the front window. One a Norwegian national flag, the other a blue-and-yellow crest with LUFC written on it.

'So,' he said as he accelerated towards the bridge to take them over the fjord to Tromsdalen and training. 'You're English?'

'We are,' Lesh said.

'I have been to England many times,' the man told them. 'I like England. I go to Leeds. I am a Leeds United fan. Lots of Norwegians follow the English football.'

'So was my dad,' Adnan said. 'A Leeds fan.'

'Good,' the driver said. 'And you are footballers too? Perhaps playing in the youth tournament?'

'We are. We beat Canada and we're playing USA in the final tomorrow.'

Hatty was the only one who didn't join in the conversation with the taxi driver. She was too anxious to talk. She knew that this training session would be hard. Not because of the physical exercise, but whether their excuses for being late, and why Lily and Kester were absent, would wash. But most of all she was worried about Georgia. Would she be able to cope with secrets?

They had decided to use the excuse that they'd been stuck in the lift in the hotel: famous now since the Prime Minister had been trapped in it. And they'd agreed to say they didn't know where the other two were. Why not? It would prove they didn't always hang out together – that they were just random members of the team like everyone else.

The taxi drew up right next to the pitch at the TUIL Arena, after bumping over some muddy tracks. Hatty, Adnan and Georgia ran on to the pitch. The rest of the England team were doing shuttle runs between cones. All except Rio, who was standing with his hands on his hips, glaring at the four latecomers, high mountains and forests towering behind him.

'You're late!' Rio shouted. 'How do you expect us

to train effectively when three of you can't make it? You were meant to meet us outside the hotel. We waited for you for ten minutes before we started.'

Rio looked at Georgia. 'And what about you, Georgia? This lot have got form for being late. But you?'

Georgia coughed. 'It's my fault they're late,' she explained.

'Is it?' Rio asked, surprised.

'Yes.'

There was a silence. Hatty wondered what Georgia would say. How could their being trapped in a lift be her fault?

'Why?' Rio looked into the taxi to see if everyone was out of the car.

'We . . .' Hatty was about to speak.

But Georgia interrupted. 'I was in a shop in Tromsø and I accidentally took a scarf without paying for it and the shop people stopped me and they would have called the police, but then Hatty turned up and sorted it out for me. I mean, she even paid for it just to stop them taking it any further, because I didn't have any money. She was really great. And the other two came down to help us. I'm really sorry, Rio.'

Hatty watched Georgia deliver a completely different excuse from the one they'd agreed with a mixture of anger and awe. The lie was completely off-script and it sounded slightly crazy, but, because of that, it was all the more believable. Also Georgia had done it by making herself look like a silly little girl, the kind of silly little girl that everyone wants to forgive. And she'd taken all the blame and painted the rest of them, especially Hatty, as her saviours.

Perfect.

It worked a treat. Johnny – who'd come over to stand by Rio – put his hand on Georgia's shoulder and smiled sympathetically.

Then Rio spoke. 'Well done, Hatty,' he said, looking confused. Hatty shrugged. She was embarrassed more than anything.

Then Johnny said, 'Where's Lily?'

'And Kester?' Rio added, looking frustrated again.

Hatty looked quickly at Georgia, to let her know that she was going to go with the excuse they'd decided on, but she paused for too long. Georgia was off. Again.

'I saw them last night. They got on that big boat that goes up the coast.'

'What?' Rio sounded horrified.

'I'm sure they'll be back for the match,' Georgia said. 'They probably think they can get away with missing training.'

'Oh, really?' said Rio.

Georgia grinned at their captain and coach.

'Well, they won't. They're dropped. They're out of the game.'

CAPTAIN'S TABLE

Kester said thank you to the waiter who'd topped up his orange juice at the captain's table. In front of him were two small slices of venison. They were red and a dribble of blood from the centre of one piece was pooling on his white plate.

He was soon served with vegetables. Carrots, thin green beans and potatoes that soaked up the blood. Kester was no longer hungry: he felt sick.

The circular table – covered in a pristine white cloth and gleaming silver cutlery – seated six people. Kester, then to his left, Frank Hawk, the ship's captain, Lily, Hawk's colleague and Marie-Ann, the woman who'd shown them round the ship, who had been invited by the captain. They sat at the centre of a wood-panelled room that seemed to belong to an older ship, not a modern liner like this.

'*Mmmmm-mmmm*,' Hawk sang. 'Venison. I love game meat. Do you kids know why it's called game?'

Kester knew, but pretended he didn't. He just glanced at the wood panelling of the captain's dining room, at the lamps fixed to the wall and the chandelier glittering above them, pretending he'd not heard the question. This was a beautiful room. Nicer than any of the public ones.

'Venison is called game because these animals can be *hunted*. And hunting is a bit like a game. Don't you think so, Captain?'

'Sometimes it can be,' the captain said with a strong Norwegian accent. 'For some people.'

'Do you hunt, Captain?' Hawk pressed.

'No. It is possible to hunt in Norway. Moose and deer, for instance. But it is not for me.'

'How about you children?' Hawk asked. 'You're English. You must have hunted for fox? Or maybe been on a grouse shoot?'

'Fox hunting's banned,' Lily said.

'Hmmm,' Hawk said. 'I heard that. What an outrage. Hunting's natural.'

Kester wanted to say that there was nothing natural about a group of people on horseback pursuing a fox, then letting their dogs rip it to pieces, but he kept quiet. He didn't need to give away his opinions on how much he hated hunting.

'You are enjoying your food?' Marie-Ann said to Lily.

Lily smiled and nodded, cutting a piece of deer meat and putting it into her mouth.

'Yes,' she said. 'Very much.'

Kester could see that Lily was not happy sitting at

this table and not happy eating an undercooked, still-bleeding deer. He felt the same. It was at times like these that he most disliked being a spy. Having to tolerate the company of people he did not like, not being able to tell them what they thought and did was wrong. But they were here to monitor Hawk. To make him think they were just normal kids. To work out if he was involved in any possible attack on Tromsø. Any personal feelings had to stay concealed. They had to tolerate anything that came at them. So they smiled as they ate with their gleaming knives and forks clinking on their large white plates.

'My favourite hunting is in Canada,' Hawk chomped as he took another large swig from his glass of wine, then reached over to refill his glass. 'Yes, there's such great hunting to be had there.'

The conversation went on. The children talked about their lives in England. Every word they said was a lie, just the cover stories they'd practised again and again. About Iris and Tom. The captain talked about the boat, Marie-Ann about people they'd put in the ship's brig. But Frank Hawk kept butting in, going on about hunting and Canada again.

'Have you been to Canada?' Kester asked the captain.

'No. Not to Canada.'

Kester realized that the captain spoke only a little

English, creating more openings for Hawk to talk. And he took them.

'Yes. Anything Canadian and I'll go after it,' Hawk said. 'Elk. Reindeer. Seal. If it's from Canada, it's game for me.'

The American stopped talking and smiled first at Kester, then Lily. Then he studied his watch and smiled again.

Kester looked across at Lily. Her face looked alarmed, like she'd just had a terrible thought. That was when Kester realized what it was.

Anything Canadian and I'll go after it. That's what he'd said. And Kester knew what he meant. *Katiyana*, Kester thought. *He's saying that he's going to kill Katiyana. Or he already has.*

And why had he looked at his watch and smiled? It meant whatever he was referring to was happening now. Right now. Maybe.

One of them had to do something. Fast.

Kester leaned back in his chair, bent forward suddenly, then vomited on to the table, across his plate and into his drink, the sharp smell of bile filling the room immediately. Being sick was a trick he'd taught himself. It never failed to send adults into a panic. A child being sick: they couldn't help themselves. So much more convincing than saying you had a stomach ache.

Every one of the adults at the table stood up in shock.

'I'm sorry, Captain,' Kester groaned. 'I'm feeling really bad. I should go and lie down. I'm really sorry.'

'No need to worry,' the captain said, looking concerned. 'Can I send a crew member with you? The ship's doctor?'

'I'll go with him,' Lily said. 'I'm so sorry. It's been lovely.'

They were running even before they were out of the captain's dining room.

At first, they dashed on to the deck to the lifeboat. A cold blast of air hit them as they raced through the door. It was dark and cold. There was rain in the air. No one else was out on the deck: the weather had turned bad.

'Do you think he's killed her?' Lily gasped.

'Maybe. No. How can he have? Not here.'

They reached the lifeboat. Kester threw back the tarpaulin on top of it. His heart was pounding so much that he thought he might really be sick.

Nothing.

No one.

'We need to check the outside deck first,' Kester shouted, his voice swallowed up by the wind. 'You go that way. I'll go this.'

They both set off to check the deck that ran round the entire circumference of the boat, Lily on the left side of the boat, Kester on the right. Front to back. At top speed. Not feeling the cold wind coming off the sea. There was no time to lose.

Less than thirty seconds later, they came together at the very back of the boat. Still nothing. But it was dark; the deck lights were not working this far back. So they looked harder. Maybe there was a reason the lights were out. And what they saw horrified them.

Two men in evening wear. Posh suits. White shirts. Between them they were heaving something over the back of the ship. Something rolled up in a sheet or a blanket.

Lily looked closer. She saw a leg and on the end of it a shoe. An unmistakable shoe. Katiyana's shoe, the same one she'd held in her hands earlier. A fur-lined boot.

As soon as the men had released their victim into the frozen, churning sea below, they turned, looking directly at Lily and Kester. Everyone seemed paralysed until they heard a distant splash, above the noise of the wind and the ship's engines. And then the men were coming at Lily and Kester, who turned to run, a bullet whizzing over their heads. They had to get away from these killers. These men who had come from nowhere.

Now.

DEAD END

'The staff door!' Kester shouted. 'From yesterday.'

He knew that if they could get down there – shutting the door behind them – they might have a chance. He could remember lots of the passageways down below.

They both heard another bullet ping off the railings as they ran for the door. Lily felt a rising panic. This was too much like that time in the desert. The last time she'd been under fire. When their old leader, Rob, had been killed. That just couldn't happen again.

They reached the door that Marie-Ann had taken them through on the tour of the ship. Kester punched in the four-digit code he'd memorized, then heaved the metal door open. Lily followed him, pushing it shut behind her.

Now what?

They were in the staff quarters, a rabbit warren of narrow corridors and steep metal stairways hidden from the passengers. That strange parallel universe onboard the ship. As they dithered, they heard a crash against the door Lily had just closed, then a series of loud cracks.

'They're shooting their way in. Trying to blow the lock,' Kester said. 'Come on!'

Lily led the way, better at remembering places than Kester. She'd mapped the ship in her mind as they'd been shown round. They ran down a staircase, then along a narrow corridor. Lily had a simple plan. Run through the busiest area in the ship where there'd be lots of crew members. That would hold the gunmen up, maybe put them off the chase. But when they hit the bottom step and turned to head towards that area of the ship they realized that one of the men was closing in on them, just fifteen or twenty metres back.

It wasn't possible. 'How?' Lily gasped. But there was no time to work it out. They had to move.

All Lily could hear was the *bang-bang-bang* of their feet as she and Kester ran down the white-painted corridor. Their assailants' footsteps too.

As they ran, the ship felt more and more like it was vibrating.

'The engine room!' Kester shouted, pointing at a doorway.

Lily burst in through the engine-room door. The bank of computers that they'd seen on their first visit was whirring and flashing. A man, sitting at a desk and examining a screen, looked up in shock. One of the engineers.

'Stop!' he said. 'Who are you?'

But Lily knew *not* to stop. If the men chasing them were willing to come into the staff area to pursue them, they'd be more than happy to come into this room and finish the job. So she ran on – Kester too – through to the engine rooms. And now the crew member was after them too.

Inside, the noise – without earplugs – was appalling. A violent, impossibly loud roaring. Lily held the door for Kester, then, as she turned to go in, she saw the crew member drop to the floor. And behind him was one of the gunmen. They'd shot the engineer. They were ruthless. Ruthless and lethal.

Lily ran on. She was going so hard now that she felt sick. The racket of the engine room, its violent noise, its flashing sparks, the adrenalin rushing through her body. It was all too much. Once she was halfway through the engine room, she found the staircase that she was looking for. But it was steep, so steep. She descended almost like a fireman down a pole, clinging to the banisters on either side. And Kester did the same.

The floor above – the one that they'd just run across – was a metal grille. Lily could see through it to the two men above them and that was bad. Because the men could see her too. Through the grille. One of them shouted, his mouth opening and closing, but his voice was drowned out by the riot of noise the engines were producing. Then he pointed the gun down at them.

This is it, Lily thought, still moving. *We'll be rolled up in a blanket like Katiyana and tossed over the side of the ship with the poor engineer.*

The next thing Lily and Kester saw was a flash and the gunman dropping to his knees above them. A shower of blood poured through the grille floor. He'd fired at them, but missed, the bullet ricocheting off some part of the engine room at him, smashing into his leg.

A piece of luck.

A small victory.

Lily and Kester set off again. To another door. A door with a code. A code Kester remembered too. They'd gained time. Seconds that might help save their lives.

Lily ran harder now. Up another tight metal staircase. Through a pair of doors. Past three of the crew, who seemed so shocked they let them pass, and outside. The cold again. The dark night again. Next to a ladder that led up to the massive ship's chimney that was spewing out dark smoke.

'The lifeboat!' Kester shouted.

'No,' Lily replied, the wind snatching her breath. 'Too obvious . . . ladder up the side of this . . . Up here . . .'

*

Only when Lily and Kester reached the far side of the chimney – that was letting out fumes and steam from the engines – did they start to breathe properly. Deep breaths, gasping in the smoky air. Neither spoke. They were listening for the second gunman. They waited until they heard him run past, mercifully missing their ladder.

The night was darkening now, little drops of wetness landing on their arms and faces. Shafts of light from windows and doorways on the ship illuminated tiny flecks of white.

Snow.

Kester and Lily sat in silence, their eyes staring into the black water. This was the first chance they'd had to speak properly since they'd seen Katiyana's body flung off the ship.

'They killed her,' Lily said eventually.

Kester nodded. 'I know.'

There was a long pause.

'What do we do now?' Lily asked. 'Where did those two men come from? We don't know who's on Hawk's side. We don't know anything or anyone.'

'Should we text Lesh?'

'No. They could intercept it.'

Kester stared out into the cloud of snow that was gusting along the fjords. Snow, for Kester, had always meant things like Christmas and sledging with his parents. Not this sense of catastrophe.

He felt desperate. 'We have to get back to Tromsø.'

Lily leaned forward. 'We do,' she agreed. 'This whole thing on the boat was to get us out of Tromsø, like they knew about us all along. So that something big can happen. Something we haven't a clue about – and that the others don't know about either.'

GHOSTS

Lily and Kester sat on the top deck of the ship with their backs to the funnel of the ship, a huge black chimney as big as a house. It was a freezing cold night, but the chimney was warm, heating their bodies through their clothes.

The snow was heavier now, swirling around in the light coming off the ship.

'We'll stay up here until we reach the next port,' Kester said, watching his breath twist away in trails as the ship passed through the black water of the night.

'Yes,' Lily agreed.

'Once we're off the ship, we can contact the others. I don't think we'll achieve anything by taking risks communicating now.'

'Do you think we could have done more to help her?' Lily asked.

'Katiyana?'

'Yes.'

Kester shook his head. 'No,' he said.

They both sat in silence. There was nothing else to say. But they were thinking about her. The girl from Canada that they hardly knew.

The night was strange. It stopped snowing after an hour. They could see for miles in every direction. Miles of sea and mountains and glaciers, a pale, cold light around the rim of the world.

Lily shivered. But not because she was cold. There was something about being on a ship in this vast world of sea and ice and rock. Something that made her feel like she wasn't in the real world at all. It was as if all the mountains were ghosts of mountains and the sea was the ghost of a sea. Or that she was a ghost.

Lily looked at her hands. She'd always imagined that being out in nature like this would be exhilarating. But it was quite the opposite.

'Do you ever think much about the last mission?' she asked quietly.

'All the time,' Kester replied.

'So why don't you talk about it?'

'Mostly we're with Lesh,' Kester said. 'And he's asked me not to. He hates all the pity he gets.'

'Yes.' Lily nodded. 'He's said the same to me. But he never talks about Jim either. Does he to you?'

'No.'

'You'd think he'd blame Jim. For the accident, I mean. If Jim hadn't . . .' Lily paused.

'. . . betrayed us?' Kester finished her sentence.

'Yes. If he'd not been such a . . . you know what, then we'd not have been in the church and Lesh wouldn't have fallen and broken his back.'

Kester was about to reply when a group of people emerged from inside the ship on to the deck. A family. Two children – much younger than Kester and Lily – were laughing and shrieking. Their parents were trying to keep them from the edge. Then, after a few minutes in the cold, they returned inside. To the warmth and light of the cafes and cabins.

Lily frowned. Seeing families always made her frown, always made her think of her mum and dad. Her dad. He'd have loved it here. He'd have taken to the mountains in his running shoes. And she'd have joined him. She closed her eyes.

'What are we doing here?' she asked, her eyes still shut.

'Up this chimney?' Kester smiled wryly.

'You know what I mean. Here – doing all of this.'

Kester didn't reply right away. *He's thinking up a good answer*, Lily thought. *Thinking of something to say that'll make me feel better, but that's still true.*

'Because we don't have parents? So we can?' he suggested.

'Hmmm.'

'Because we don't have families and because they were taken away from us by people who want to cause havoc in the world and don't care about a girl like you losing her father and mother . . .'

Lily interrupted Kester at this point, '. . . and we do all this to stop that happening again to other children.'

'That's right,' Kester said.

'It's a good enough reason,' Lily added.

'Except Adnan has the chance to have a family now,' Kester said.

'He does.'

'I've not been able to talk to him about it for a couple of days,' Kester went on. 'I think he's putting it off until after the mission, but I'd say he wants a family.'

'What did he say?'

'That he wanted it,' Kester said. 'But also that he'd miss us and what we do.'

'What do you think he'll do?'

'Well, what would you tell him to do?' Kester pressed.

Lily didn't hesitate. 'Go back. Be with a family. If he can.'

As the two children spoke, the *Nordlys* pushed on through the black waves, heading to the northernmost tip of the European land mass.

Alongside the ship, a pair of whales moved invisibly with them.

THURSDAY

COLD TOWN

As the sun came up fully the next morning – its rays reflecting off the blanket of white that covered the Arctic scenery of northern Norway – the *Nordlys* moved gently into the harbour of a port.

Hammerfest was a small town. No more than a few hundred houses shivering with cold underneath a pair of mountains and a gigantic glacier wedged between them. The port was a nondescript row of ageing three-storey office blocks. Unremarkable. Empty. Bleak. And around it miles and miles of snow and rock.

They were now as far north as you could go on mainland Europe.

Once the boat had docked, two electronic ramps dropped down. The larger one was to allow a truck to leave the ship, chains attached to its tyres to help it grip the roads. The smaller ramp was lowered to let the crew and a few passengers on to the harbourside. Some of those passengers stood holding up their cameras, capturing the spectacular scenery, stamping their feet in the fresh snow. Others were met by locals. But it was early. There were really very few people about and those who were disappeared quickly, climbing into cars and vans to escape the bitter cold.

Two other people – at the back of this group – moved purposefully off the ship, wrapped up in coats, hoods up, heads down, looking like they knew exactly where they were going. They moved past a crane that was lifting wooden boxes on to the back of the ship, then round the back of a painted wooden building, out of sight of the great ship.

Lily and Kester stopped and pulled their hoods away from their faces.

'Shall we contact the others now?' Lily asked.

'Let's wait until the ship goes,' Kester replied. 'In case anyone could intercept us.'

Lily frowned and wished the boat would hurry up and leave so that they could warn Lesh, Hatty and Adnan. Warn them that it was the American who was causing trouble – not the Russian – and that they were sure something was going to happen in Tromsø. Soon.

They both kept watch on the boat from behind the wooden building. No one had disembarked after them. Certainly not Hawk. Everyone else who'd left the boat had returned up the ramp. The only other thing that had disembarked was the truck – and that was long gone. Eventually, the ship sounded its horn.

More deep booms echoing off the mountains, announcing its departure. Then it began to move away, slowly at first, churning its great propeller to reverse a little before heading out into the fjord.

Lily looked from the boat to the small town they'd arrived at. She knew about it because she'd read up about every town in the area on the plane coming into Norway, as well as the transport links between those towns. And, because of that, she knew that the main way of getting in and out of Hammerfest was by the Hurtigruten, even more so now as winter approached. Once the snow set in, many of the roads in the area became impassable, often for the whole of the winter.

The boat had almost gone round the corner of the fjord now. The pair walked to the front of the wooden building to watch it disappear behind the headland, a wind coming off the water.

'I thought there'd be a police car or something,' Lily said.

'Me too.'

'I mean, don't you think they found the injured crew member – or did they miss the gunshots?'

'It was noisy in the engine room. Perhaps they concealed the body. If they killed him.'

'Let's text Lesh,' Lily said, feeling suddenly uneasy, like she wanted to be away from this town, even though they'd only been there minutes. 'It's safe to now.'

'Not as safe as you'd like to think,' said a third voice. An American voice.

Kester and Lily turned in horror to see the silhouettes of two men behind them. They'd emerged from where Lily and Kester had just come from. It was two men they knew well. Frank Hawk and one of Katiyana's killers from the night before. Both holding rifles.

For a few seconds neither of the Americans spoke. Hawk was smiling. Almost laughing. He was watching them, waiting for them to make the next move.

Lily took the time to glance around her. There was neither sight nor sound of anyone else. She wondered if this was an inhabited town at all. It looked more like a set of concrete boxes that people had abandoned, left empty for the entire winter. Perhaps forever.

The situation was stark. They were alone. They were unarmed. So they had no option but to do what they were told by the Americans.

'Move,' the second American said eventually, pointing to the far end of the harbour.

Lily and Kester glanced at each other, sharing a sense of hopelessness rather than fear. They walked along the edge of the harbour on to a path that led round the side of a huge rock. Lily placed her feet carefully as the snow was fresh. Then she wondered why she was bothering. What did it matter if she slipped and fell? Weren't they being taken away from the buildings to be killed? Just like Katiyana had been. She kept her mind alive and alert for any chance to escape this situation. She knew Kester would be doing the same.

Never surrender.

They walked for fifteen minutes, even passing reindeer eating vegetation, unworried by this small group of people walking by.

'You're not terribly effective spies, are you, kids?'

Neither Lily nor Kester answered.

'I mean,' Hawk went on, 'it almost seems a shame to do this to you. We've led you all the way. This trip, for instance. You followed us because you thought we were heading out to trigger a nuclear device. Didn't you?'

No reply.

'You did. You listened in on the bug in my hat. The hat I left on the top of the cable car mountain. You put all your resources into investigating some Russian ecologist who wouldn't know a spy from a skylark.' The American laughed. 'Because of some papers we left in his hotel room. But do you know how we knew who you were?'

Lily, like Kester, remained quiet.

'Go silent to your graves if you like,' Hawk said in a darker voice, 'but I'll tell you anyway. When you were in my room that night, when I came back in up a secret way I know. Well, I needed to know who you were, but not for you to know I knew. So I sprayed you – as you hid behind that sofa – with a chemical that showed up on your clothes when I saw you in the bar. I shone a laser on you and knew immediately you were the ones.'

'The ones we had to kill,' the second American said.

'I liked you two,' Hawk said, ignoring his colleague, and he looked genuinely disappointed. 'But needs must.'

'Needs must what?' Lily asked, speaking at last, her voice hard. She was shivering now, because they'd stopped walking. But Hawk wasn't listening. He was staring up at the mountains above Hammerfest.

'Look at that,' he said. 'A beautiful wilderness. Doesn't it look beautiful to you, kids?'

Lily said nothing. She just stared at the unforgiving emptiness of rock and snow and ice. It looked anything but beautiful at this moment. It looked desolate. It looked dead.

'Do you know, that whole business with that Canadian girl, it troubled me,' Hawk said. 'Because . . . because it was too easy. *Bang bang*, she's dead. It just doesn't seem fair. You wouldn't do that with one of these reindeer, would you? You'd chase it a bit, give it a chance, or at least make it *think* it had a chance. And, deep down, not know for sure you were going to catch it. Hunting. That's what I'm talking about. So, kids, I'm going to give *you* a sporting chance.'

Hawk suddenly dropped his rifle at his side. 'You have half an hour.'

Lily and Kester couldn't believe what they were hearing. Hawk was telling them that they could go. And that he was hunting them.

It was sick.

It was terrifying.

But it meant they had a chance.

HUMAN PREY

To conserve energy, Lily and Kester ran at a steady pace, putting some distance between them and the two Americans. They just hoped he'd stick to his word and give them half an hour.

At first, escaping was simple. The snow on the lower ground was less than two centimetres deep and covering only soft grass or earth. Easy running, if a little slippery. But, as they climbed higher up the steep, sloping sides of the fjord, the snow became deeper. Five centimetres. Ten centimetres. More.

Deeper snow would not have been a problem, except that the terrain underfoot was not flat earth or grass. Now it was scree: small- and medium-sized pieces of rock scattered on the sides of the mountains. The pair moved carefully, keeping on all fours to avoid a fall that might lead to an injury that would slow them down disastrously. Neither of them was wearing gloves and soon they felt the same kind of cold burning sensation you feel after you've been snowballing with bare hands.

Neither Lily nor Kester spoke as they ran. What they needed to do was simple: get away from Hawk as quickly as possible. They'd seen what his accomplices had done to Katiyana. They both knew the form without speaking about it.

If you were being pursued up a hill, you didn't just run up the side. If you did, you could be tracked from a single point. That is why they were running *around* the hill at the same time as ascending. That meant they could use the side of the mountain as cover.

After ten minutes of climbing, Kester stopped by an outcrop of rocks. 'Just give me a minute,' he said. 'And . . . and we need to work out what to do.'

'Get away,' Lily said. 'That's it. Come on.'

'But where to?'

'Away,' Lily said anxiously. But she knew she had to be careful. Kester was not used to running up hills in ice and snow. And she was.

'But why didn't he just kill us?' Kester asked.

As he asked Lily the question, the answer came immediately into his mind. He remembered sitting at the captain's table onboard the ship and Hawk saying how much he loved hunting. That he'd hunt anything. How had he put it? *Hunting is a bit like a game. Don't you think so, Captain?* Something like that.

'He's hunting us,' Kester said.

'What?'

'He's hunting us like he would animals. Like he hunts deer and whatever. He said he loves to hunt new creatures all the time. They make it more interesting. The sport. We're his prey. It's like a game to him. And he's all the more excited because we're human prey.'

Lily wiped the sweat from her forehead. Kester was right. 'So we need to get away,' she said. 'And as fast as possible. Without leaving tracks.'

'Come on then,' Kester said.

They both fell backwards and hit the ground when they heard it. The crack of a bullet hitting the heap of rocks they were leaning on. When the second bullet came, they rolled behind the larger rock. Kester peered briefly over the top, then ducked as another bullet ricocheted off the rock.

'Where's he firing from?' Lily asked.

'He's at the foot of the hill. Five minutes behind us, I'd say. They're kneeling and firing.'

'That's not half an hour. He's only given us ten minutes.'

Kester looked again and saw that the two figures had stopped firing and were climbing.

'Come on!' he shouted. 'Ten minutes are better than nothing. They're moving again, not shooting. The hill flattens out soon. If we make it up there, we have a chance.'

So they ran.

Faster now.

A burst of speed that took them to the top of the hill and – mercifully – out of the firing line.

'Now what?' Kester asked.

The top of the hill was a vast plateau, leading to a gradual slope heading up to a cairn – a two-metre pile of rocks – overlooking the water. A strong wind was whistling across the open spaces. What must have been a rugged landscape with plenty of possible hiding places was now like a blank sheet, apart from the cairn. Every footstep they made could be seen up close. And another person or animal would be visible from kilometres away, black against the pure white.

'We can't go across here,' Lily muttered. 'Once he's up top, he'll see us for miles.'

'And we can't go down,' Kester urged. 'He'll see us if we do that too.'

They stared out across the vast expanse of white and both spoke at the same time, as they felt a sudden shower of snow rushing in at them from the north.

'We need to hide.'

They could hear the crunch of both men's boots clearly as they crouched low. How had the Americans found them already?

'No sign,' Hawk's sidekick said.

'That's because they're good,' Hawk replied, eyeing the cairn, with snow packed into its crevices. 'I love it. Intelligent prey.'

'So what now, sir?'

'We head to the top. We can see everything from the top once this snow calms down. There's some tough weather coming in. Look, there's a mountain hut there. They might even be in there. Then we wait.'

When the footsteps had gone, Lily moved half a dozen stones out of her way and peered across the hill to see if their hunters really were going.

'They're moving away,' she said to Kester. 'We're covered on this side.'

Kester moved some stones out of his way and stretched his legs. They'd been hiding in the cairn or a part of it. They'd removed several stones, covered themselves with some of them, and in five minutes the drifting snow had hidden them and the stones they'd moved from view.

'That was a good idea, Kester,' Lily said with a smile.

'It was.' Kester grimaced. 'Let's head back down.'

'No. Not down,' Lily said grimly.

'What?'

'Not down.'

'Why not?' Kester asked.

'Well, what's the point in that? If we go, we'll lose him. He might be hunting us – and that means we should try to escape. But we're also spying on him. We need to find out what he's up to. Look, the weather's closing in. He might think he's lost us. We've got the advantage back.'

Kester knew that Lily was right. They didn't have to get as far *away* as possible from Hawk as they could. They had to get *close* to him. Really close.

And that meant going on.

'OK,' Kester said. 'I agree. But first, let's text Lesh.'

Less than ten kilometres away, only a few metres below the surface of the fjords around Hammerfest in a state-of-the-art submarine, a man with a headset on was sitting at a computer.

When his machine began to bleep, he looked at the screen and read what was on there.

> LHA.
>
> WE ARE PURSUING TARGET 2.
>
> HAMMERFEST HILLS.
>
> LK

The man took his headphones off and smiled. 'Sir. I have their position,' he said.

'Good,' said a tall, athletic-looking man. 'Good. Let's go and find them.'

STORM

The wind was driving patchy snow in at high speed over the mountains now, making it hard for Lily and Kester to walk. Their outdoor gear was of the highest quality, but they could still feel the wetness of the snow and the cold on their necks and hands. The cold was seeping in through every gap in their clothing.

It was freezing. Visibility was poor. Sometimes they could see for kilometres, sometimes metres, the mountains appearing and disappearing in waves of snow.

The storm was good news for them in other ways. The mountain top was so wild now that the Americans had holed up in the hut, forced to give up the hunt for the two children.

Approaching the hut, Kester signalled that they should go round the back, so they wouldn't be seen as they came closer. There was little chance of this, as the small wooden door was closed and the snow was very thick. It was a tiny hut, smaller than a garage that you could drive one car into. From the back it looked more like a pile of stones, huge snowdrifts smoothing its sides.

Kester moved close to Lily and whispered in her ear, the wind obscuring his words from anyone but her.

'Can we listen in on what they're saying? Is there any way?'

Lily looked at the structure of the hut. It was not built like a modern building. It was more like a drystone wall. No mortar, just stones carefully placed to keep out the snow and the cold. She tried to clear her head, to ignore the weather conditions that were making it so hard for her to think. It didn't take long to work out a solution.

Lily grabbed Kester's head and spoke into his ear. 'I could use a bug and feed it through some of the stones,' she said. 'If it got far enough into the wall, we might be able to pick up what they're saying.'

Kester smiled. 'Do it. Do whatever it takes, without giving ourselves away,' he said. 'What do you need?'

'A piece of wire and this listening device,' Lily said. 'That's all.'

After a pause, Kester grinned again. 'I've got just the thing.'

It took him ten minutes. He had to take his rucksack apart, strip the canvas from it and unpick the stitching, all without gloves, his hands frozen and wet because of the driving snow. But there, after all his efforts, from the structure of the rucksack, was a thirty-centimetre piece of wire.

'Perfect,' Lily said, emerging from her hood, the wind and snow stinging her face.

Once she'd attached the pin-sized listening device to Kester's wire, Lily began to feed it into the wall of the mountain hut. Kester put in an earpiece and listened to the sound of the bug as it hit stones and rubble inside the wall. He also kept an eye on the front of the hut. If this went wrong, then the Americans could be out and on to them in seconds.

'The walls must be a half a metre thick,' Lily spoke into Kester's ear as the howling of the wind seemed to be picking up. 'Can you hear anything yet?'

Kester shook his head. He'd noticed that Lily's teeth were chattering. She was very cold. They'd been stationary for more than fifteen minutes now. Kester adjusted his earpiece to get the best sound he could. And there, at last, he heard voices. He signalled to Lily to stop. Her bug was within range. The plan had worked.

'We need to move on. Find those kids.' It was the second American's voice.

'It's too wild out there,' Hawk replied. 'We have to sit this out. So do they. They won't be going anywhere. Anyway, my worry is the device.'

Kester held his breath. The device? Was Hawk about to talk about the warhead?

'When does it come in?'

'Tomorrow,' Hawk answered.

'Is it primed?'

'It is.'

'And will you let it . . . you know . . .'

'What do you think?'

'No. I think you're using it to set up the Russian. Make everyone think he's trying to destabilize things.'

'That's true in part,' Hawk said. 'I want Russia blamed. And it wouldn't just be a war between us and the Russians. It'd be the world against the Russians. And, once they were on their knees, who would get access to all their oil?'

'We would, sir.'

'Exactly.'

'So when?'

'Tomorrow. Tomorrow afternoon.'

Hawk paused. 'Don't look so worried,' he said, laughing.

'Just how powerful is this thing?' the second American asked.

'It'll kill everyone in Tromsø immediately. Then most people within twenty kilometres will suffer radiation poisoning and die in a year or two.'

'What about the heads of state? The British Prime Minister, for instance.'

'Dead too. And it'll be no loss. He's weak. He even said he doesn't like war.'

'That's a lot of dead,' the second American said. 'Men, women and children.'

'Correct.' Hawk chuckled. 'Whales too. Seals. All sorts of creatures. This place will be a radioactive desert for decades. And all caused by me tip-tapping a code into this.'

'What code?'

'My secret code.'

'Which is?'

'Which is something in my head, not written down.'

There was a pause, during which Lily and Kester eyed each other in alarm at what they were hearing. Then Frank Hawk spoke again. 'Don't worry. I'll make sure you're safe. After the soccer game tomorrow, we'll get away. I've got all the equipment we need to survive.'

As the two Americans spoke, Kester and Lily looked at each other in full understanding. They knew Hawk's plan. They knew it would be the worst terrorist atrocity ever committed and that it would have knock-on effects for generations. They also knew that they had to put their lives on the line to make sure it didn't happen.

THE FALL

'Must get back to Tromsø,' Kester said, barely able to speak now that the wind was so strong, driving sharp pieces of ice into his eyes.

'Yes,' Lily said. 'Hammerfest first. It's going to be hard.'

'No choice,' Kester responded. 'The alternative is too terrible.'

They stopped listening to the Americans and quickly put the wreckage of Kester's rucksack into Lily's. They had to hold on to everything they had, just in case.

If they'd carried on listening for a little longer, they would have had warning. Warning that the Americans had made the same decision as them. To head back to Tromsø. Their hunters were right on their tail.

Lily and Kester scrambled down a slope, then picked their way across great fields of rocks. It was heavy-going and very slow. But this was their only option. Although the snow was lighter now, the air around them was so uniformly white that it was impossible to navigate by choosing landmarks, so Kester used the compass he'd retrieved from his rucksack. North-west across the wide open space until they reached the edge of the mountain. Then a steep drop down to the water.

They walked slowly, much slower than a normal person walking down a normal street. But above them the clouds moved swiftly across the sky. And, as the clouds moved, the snow stopped. They could see rock formations now. A glimpse, through the low cloud, of water below.

'That's good,' Kester said, glancing at Lily.

But Lily didn't look like she thought anything was good: she was frowning, squinting hard across the fields of snow behind her.

Kester followed her line of sight and saw them. Two black figures against the perfect white. Less than five hundred metres away. One was pointing. The other was bending down, pulling something from a bag.

A gun.

The hunters were after them again.

'Run,' Kester shouted, heading out across the open fields to their right.

'No,' Lily shouted back, looking down the steep slope that fell away to their left. 'We're easy meat if we go that way. We have to go down.'

As if to reinforce what she'd said, a bullet slammed into the rocks next to Kester.

'Too steep,' Kester shouted.

'No choice,' Lily replied, diving down the slope. Kester had no option but to go straight after her.

They descended at high speed, skimming the surface of the snow, legs first. At first, they had just been falling, but within seconds the pair were using their legs to steer as they fell, avoiding sticking out bits of rock, trying to keep to the smooth snow, digging in their feet to keep the speed down. It was a bit like sledging without a sledge. Or sledging using your body as the sledge. That was the half-thought that passed through Lily's mind. The only half-thought she allowed herself.

The drop was over a kilometre. A high, steep hill descended in under a minute. Dangerous and deadly. Painful. Physical. Thrilling. Almost like skydiving, but without the sky.

Soon they found themselves closing in on the bottom of the hill and the freezing water below. And freezing water might have been OK. But this freezing water was full of sharp rocks that they could quite easily break a leg on – or worse.

Kester forced his legs deep into the snow in a bid to stop, then looked across at Lily. She was doing the same. And it started to work. They *were* slowing down. They both dug their legs in even deeper.

The events of the next few seconds passed so

quickly, neither Lily nor Kester could do anything about it. As they slowed at the foot of the mountain, just before the water, feeling they were safe at last, they shared a grim smile. Until, that is, they saw two things that surprised them.

First, a shape in the water like a whale, a tower emerging from it. They both knew immediately it was a submarine.

Second, three large men waiting at the foot of the hill by the water.

Lily and Kester could do nothing but carry on sliding slowly downhill towards the men, however much they dug their heels in. The men grabbed them without a word, put hands over their mouths and dragged them beneath some overhanging rocks. That's when things became even more alarming.

The men took off the children's storm jackets, wrapped the jackets round two medium-sized tree trunks and flung the jacketed trunks into the water below. Lily and Kester watched in horror as the floating jackets were riddled with bullets, cracks of gunfire chasing the bullets down the slope. Hawk and his sidekick fired at least ten bullets into each of the logs, from their hilltop position a kilometre higher up. Only when the firing stopped did Kester and Lily look up from the overhang to see their new captors.

Two of the men were strangers.

The other was Jim Sells.

Jim Sells. Their coach and ex-commander from their last mission. A former England footballer. A former spy for the UK, now an operative for Russia. The man who had betrayed them just months ago.

JIM

'You!' Lily hissed when the firing had stopped.

'Hello, Lily. Hello, Kester.' Jim Sells's voice sounded calm and kind. Just like it used to. And nothing like it should do on this most dangerous of occasions. 'It looks like your friends think you're dead and drowned,' he added.

The two men with him moved into position at the end of the overhang, checking to see what the Americans at the top of the hill were doing. 'They're long gone, sir,' one said in Russian.

Lily watched them and – understanding what they said – she launched herself at Jim, cracking the side of his head hard with her fist. Then his shoulder and chest. She finished with a punch to his mouth. Jim did nothing to stop her. He took the blows. He didn't even turn away.

Kester stood and watched. He'd never seen Lily so violent. But he understood that she needed to do what she was doing, even though she'd also know that it would have little impact on a man like Jim. He remembered how, at first, Jim had been a hero to them. An ex-footballer. An experienced spy. He'd run their mission in Poland – and, then, at the last minute, had betrayed them, siding with a group of Russians who were trying to murder the entire England team.

When Lily had stopped hitting him, Jim spoke again. 'I'm sorry,' he said.

'You're a traitor,' Lily spat.

'I am,' Jim nodded. 'I am a traitor. To the UK. And I'm sorry you had to be dragged into all that. I never expected a group of children to get in our way. That's why I sent you away from Krakow. To the lake. That's why I tried to get the helicopter to leave you there, so you'd not be in danger in the city. But you survived. And you stopped us. Through your own skill.'

'Survived? But we didn't, did we?' Lily said. 'Lesh didn't survive. Do you know about Lesh?'

'I know he can't walk,' Jim said. 'And I'm deeply sorry about that.'

Lily wanted to use every swear word she'd ever heard and hurl them at Jim. She racked her brains to find something she could say to hurt him. He was the one of the few adults she had trusted – even cared about – since the death of her parents. And he had utterly betrayed her. But now, as her anger dissipated, she was thinking, aware that they were at the foot of this snowy mountain, next to what she assumed was a Russian submarine.

What is Jim doing here? Now? On this randomly distant shoreline in the snow. How is he involved?

Kester and Lily's silence drew a question from Jim. 'You want to know why I'm here?' he asked.

But, before Kester could answer, one of Jim's men returned from their reconnaissance.

'The Americans headed back to the town,' he said in Russian. Lily repeated it in English for Kester.

'Good,' Jim said, looking at Lily. 'They think you're dead. They think that you fell in the water after coming down the hill and that they put ten rounds into each of you. They've underestimated the two of you.'

'And *are* we dead?' Kester said, speaking at last, ignoring the compliment.

Jim put his hand on Kester's shoulder. But Kester shrugged it off. Jim frowned. 'You think we're here to kill you?'

'I don't know what to expect,' Kester replied. 'You've only ever lied to us.'

'Fair point,' Jim said.

'So what are you doing here?' Lily asked.

'I've come to help you.'

'Help us. That's a joke.'

'Lily, I just saved your lives.'

'You could save my life a thousand times before I

say thank you, after what you did to Lesh. After all the lies.'

'Lily? Can I ask you something?'

'If you have to,' Lily said, staring out across the fjord, a dark snow cloud scudding in, the water choppier now.

'Are you comfortable lying to Johnny, Rio and the others? Because, if I remember correctly, you lie to them all the time . . .'

'We lie!' Lily sputtered. 'Yes, we lie. But we lie because we're trying to do good.' She stood up and was shouting now. 'Don't try and say we're like you. We're not. You're bad. We're good.'

'Why are you good?'

'Because we try to stop people doing bad things to British people and you try to do bad things *to* British people.'

'Maybe I do,' Jim said. 'But I try to do good things *for* Russian people. Why is it that the British are always right and the Russians wrong?'

'It's not like that,' Lily growled back. 'We simply try to stop things like twenty-two young men, some of them fathers, getting murdered. Remember? That's what you tried to do.'

'It's more complex than that,' Jim said, deflecting Lily's reference to their last mission. 'I'll explain it to you one day.'

'Explain it now. I challenge you.'

'Russia is like my home now,' Jim said. 'The

people. Their way of life. In the past there was something good about it, although everyone else thought it was a bad place . . .'

'Forget it,' Lily said, putting her hands up. 'We have better things to do than sit around listening to more of your lies. We're trying to stop . . .' She silenced herself, remembering the mission they were on now.

'. . . trying to stop what?' Jim laughed. 'A third world war? A warhead going off. The Russians getting blamed for it all when it's the Americans who are behind it?'

'Forget it,' Lily said, realizing that Jim knew exactly what their mission was and that he had just confirmed that everything they'd worked out was true, meaning that he was at least one step ahead of the Squad. 'We're leaving. If, that is, it's true you're not going to kill us.'

'Do you want a lift?' Jim asked.

'In that?' Lily gestured towards the submarine.

'Yes.' Jim grinned.

Kester stepped forward. 'No, thank you,' he said.

'So how are you going to get back to Tromsø by the morning?' Jim asked. 'You have only one option. Come with us. In this.'

Lily looked at the submarine tower shifting slowly in the waters, then at Kester.

'Maybe we should,' Kester said, changing his mind. 'It's not like we have a choice.'

'What?' Lily said. 'Accept a lift with him. He almost got us killed the last time he lied to us. What's to say he's not going to take us out there and kill us?'

'Lily. If I wanted to kill you, you'd be at the bottom of that fjord already.'

UNDERWATER

Kester slept for most of the journey.

Lily looked at him lying there. How could he sleep at a time like this? She was shattered too, but there was no way she could sleep at such a key point in a mission. And – added to that – they were travelling underwater at sixty kilometres an hour in a Russian submarine with a man who once left them to die.

Lily grimaced. She knew that as spies they had to concentrate on what their goal was – stopping the attack on Tromsø – and not how they went about reaching it. But she wasn't happy. She gazed round the room she was in. Or was it a cabin? It was small with white walls, a table in the middle and six chairs around the table. A sofa at the side. She could have been in a normal staffroom in a normal building like a school, not a submarine at all.

Being in this underwater ship – which is really what it was – was even stranger than Lily could have imagined. The insides were packed with pipes and wires strapped to the ceiling. At one end of the submarine there was a small room with three men in it, all looking at screens, headphones on. The doorways along the length of the submarine were the most unusual thing: they were round and had rubber around their edges. Lily knew what this meant. If one part of the submarine became flooded, they could close one of these doors and it would act as a seal.

The most striking feeling about the submarine, though, was the claustrophobia, the sense of being in an enclosed space with no way out. This was caused by the small rooms, the lack of space and the low ceilings. Not to mention the fact that they were submerged under several metres of water.

Lily heard footsteps behind her, breaking her train of thought about the submarine.

Jim.

Lily glanced at him and back at Kester, who was still sleeping.

'I need to tell you something about Frank Hawk,' Jim said.

'Forget it,' Lily said.

'It's important.'

'Why should I trust anything you say?' Lily asked.

'I'm sure you won't,' Jim said. 'But I'll tell you anyway.' Lily shrugged, still looking away from Jim.

Jim sat down at the table. 'Spying isn't black and white,' he said.

'No?'

'It's complicated, that's all. One minute someone can seem to have betrayed you and have caused your friend to be crippled. The next minute he can go out of his way to save your life and give you a piece in a jigsaw that can help you stop a major war.'

Finally, Lily looked at Jim. 'So, if you know what the piece in the jigsaw is, why don't *you* save the world?'

'Just listen, OK?'

'OK.'

'I don't know all the details about your mission.' Jim paused. 'And I don't expect you to tell me them. But we do know something.'

'Yes?'

'We know that Hawk is planning something.' Jim's face clouded over, serious. 'But we also know that he has a weakness.'

'And that is?'

'He wants the USA to win the football.'

'How would you know that?'

'We've been listening to his conversations.'

'His conversations with who?'

'With his grandchildren. Just like you've been listening. And he's been boasting to them about how the USA team is going to beat England. He wants the USA to win the football. He wants you to lose tomorrow. Only after that has happened is he going to do whatever it is you think he's going to do.'

After Lily had remained silent for a few seconds,

she finally spoke. 'Thank you,' she said. 'That could be useful.'

'You're welcome,' Jim smiled.

Lily couldn't think of anything to say after that, so she said nothing.

Then Jim cleared his throat. 'Even though I did what I did, Lily,' he said, 'I always thought the world of you.'

Lily turned and stared straight into Jim's face. 'I thought the world of you too – up until you did what you did,' she replied, feeling her eyes go red and hot. She swallowed and gritted her teeth. Jim nodded in response to what she'd said. And Lily could see that she had – at last – wounded him.

But it didn't make her feel any better.

They stayed together in silence. Lily sitting. Jim standing. Until Jim walked down the corridor of the submarine without adding anything more.

Lily sat at the table with her eyes closed as the submarine cut on through the water, speeding towards Tromsø.

Thinking.

Thinking for what seemed like hours.

Thinking about Jim, about the Squad and about her mum and dad.

What was she doing on this submarine, trusting someone who had so utterly betrayed them, heading to a city where a nuclear bomb might be about to go off? Why was it down to her and her friends to stop it?

She thought of the mission in the desert where Rob had been killed.

Why had that happened?

She thought of finding Lesh at the foot of a tower after they'd stopped the England football team being attacked.

Why had they been involved in that?

She thought of looking over her shoulder on the lake that day, seeing her parents – all their parents – murdered.

Then she had her answer. It always came back to that.

She had lost her mum and dad.

She had lost everything.

Therefore, she had nothing.

So she was going to make sure no other children had to suffer that. She and the Squad. In memory of their parents. Because doing something about that was better than just feeling sorry for yourself.

Frank Hawk was back in Tromsø within two hours of leaving the mountain top. He'd called in a helicopter and made swift progress back to the scene of his planned crime.

As he descended to Tromsø airport, he smiled to see a small fishing boat edging up the fjord.

'That's it,' he said to his sidekick.

'What?'

'The warhead, you idiot. By morning I'll have it armed and primed. Ready to go off at the push of a button. But, before we fly out of here, there's the little matter of seeing the USA beat England at soccer. Should be easier now two of their players are at the bottom of that fjord.'

FRIDAY

JIGSAW PIECES

Lily and Kester walked, crunching through the snow, towards the TUIL Arena's main stand. It was dusk now. Quiet. A mist hanging on the white mountains. A skein of large black birds emerging then disappearing in the white.

Once they'd joined the rest of the Squad, Julia led them, unspeaking, into a heated room.

'OK,' she said. 'There's a lot to talk about. We've got half an hour to cover everything. We need all the details. Ready?' Everyone nodded.

'Hatty. Tell the others about Georgia.'

Hatty sighed before she started. 'Georgia sussed us,' she confessed. 'And she . . . and she . . . well, she . . . she . . . helped us rule out Esenin. The Russian.'

'How?' Lily asked.

Hatty told them the whole story. Finding Georgia with Esenin. Challenging her. Then, in the end, using her to quiz the Russian.

'So Esenin has been definitely ruled out?' Kester asked.

'He has,' Julia said. 'There's no evidence to suggest he knows anything about the warhead and the threat. Unless you have any more information?'

'We've ruled him out too,' Kester said. 'It's Hawk we need to worry about.'

'Is it?' Julia said.

'Yes.'

'Explain.'

'We listened in to him,' Lily said. 'He was in a mountain hut, in a storm. For once, I don't think he knew we were there. He was talking about a warhead. He plans to set it off today. After the game.'

'Where it is?' Julia asked, her voice deep and serious.

'We don't know that.'

'But you're sure he's planning this after the game?'

'Yes,' Lily said.

'You're absolutely sure?'

'Absolutely sure.'

'How?' Julia asked.

'Jim told us.'

'JIM?' Hatty, Lesh and Adnan's voices echoed round the room. Julia's face was calm, but interested. So Lily explained about the rescue. The hiding. The conversations.

'Hawk has some sort of device that he'll put a code into and that will set off the bomb,' she said. 'But not until after the game. And that gives us our chance.'

'So you've got a plan?' Julia frowned.

'Yes.'

'Go on.'

Lily looked at Kester. It was his job to explain the plan.

'Hawk will come to watch the game. He'll leave afterwards, setting the bomb off once he's clear. He has it on a timer. We need to separate Hawk and his assistant during the game. Then we might have a chance.'

'How?' Julia pressed.

'We lose the game,' Lily said.

'Lose the game?' Adnan asked, exasperated.

'We lose the game,' Lily repeated. 'We find a way of getting Hawk involved in the celebrations. Then we take out his assistant.'

'OK,' Julia said. 'It sounds like a plan. Now let's have some detail.'

Hatty saw Georgia in the hotel cafe an hour later. The other girl looked up at her uneasily from her drink and Hatty knew that she understood they had to talk.

Five minutes later, they were standing on the edge of the fjord together.

'We need another favour from you,' Hatty explained.

'Really?'
'Yes.'
'And what favour is that?'
'The game against the USA.'
'What about it?'
'We need you to help us lose it.'

The look on Georgia's face was a picture. And Hatty couldn't decide whether the other girl would go along with the plan or not.

ENGLAND V. USA

The England team that took to the pitch for the tournament final was depleted. There was no Lily or Kester, who had, everyone thought, disappeared off the face of the earth, meaning a major reshuffle at the back.

The small stadium was packed with 2,000 supporters. The place seemed even stranger now that it was full: this tiny field of football fans underneath steep wooded mountainside and bare rock, all covered in a magnificent blanket of snow. The only area that was not white was the pitch.

In the executive boxes towards the back of the main stand, most of the politicians who were involved in the conference were dining, all in dresses and black suits with white shirts. Feeding themselves up before the final evening of the conference. They'd been invited to the dinner to encourage them to come to the final. And to give them a chance of an international photo opportunity.

Among them, as well as the British Prime Minister, was Frank Hawk. But Hawk wasn't dressed smartly like the other politicians. He was wearing a USA football shirt.

'*U-S-A!*' he shouted as the teams came on to the pitch. '*U-S-A!*' All the Squad could hear him above the general noise of the crowd.

'Is that him?' Georgia asked Hatty as they lined up. Hatty nodded.

'This is going to be hard,' Georgia said. 'Losing on purpose, I mean.'

'It is,' Hatty agreed, her voice muted. 'But it needs doing.'

And Georgia had been right: it *was* hard to lose on purpose.

The England team were – mostly – good. The attack and midfield players were making mincemeat out of the USA team, who had no defence against the crisp passing that Rio and the others were delivering.

The first goal came from Finn and Rio. As well as being best friends off the pitch, they were close on the pitch too. A one-two from the pair cut the USA team in half and Finn was able to slot the ball home.

1–0.

This was not the plan. Not for the Squad anyway.

As the defence took their positions after the goal,

Georgia frowned at Hatty. 'What do we do?' she asked.

'Give away penalties,' Hatty said. 'I'll do one and you do one.'

'OK,' Georgia sighed.

But at half-time it was still 1–0 to England. And the England dressing room was bubbling.

'This is easy,' Rio said. 'We are so going to win this tournament. We're clearly the best.'

'So easy,' Finn echoed.

'Let's just play it safe,' Rio went on. 'Everyone? No rash tackles.'

The team nodded, drank their sports drinks, rubbed their tired muscles. They were confident – most of them – but not Hatty, Adnan or Georgia. They needed to find a way of losing this match. They had to lose it. If they won, the consequences were terrifying.

When the referee knocked on their door, they went back out on to the pitch for the second half.

Ten minutes into the second half, Hatty chopped an American girl in the penalty area. Adnan made it easy for her by staying on his goal line to create confusion in the box.

From the stand a huge shout went up. 'PENALTY!'

Hawk.

The referee blew his whistle and pointed at the

spot. Hatty, who'd fallen over while making the tackle, was helped to her feet by Rio.

'Hard luck, Hatty. You couldn't do much else.'

Hatty smiled sheepishly. But then she noticed the referee was facing her, standing by the penalty spot, a red card in his hand, raised high. The USA fans cheered again. Hatty was off, England down to ten players.

Hatty stormed off the pitch, purposely walking past Georgia. 'It's up to you,' Hatty muttered.

'I know,' the other girl snapped.

'You need to make us lose this,' Hatty pushed. 'You and Adnan.'

'I know. I told you.'

And for the first time Hatty saw that Georgia looked vulnerable. She knew she had to make her feel strong, so that she could deliver.

'Look, Georgia,' she said. 'I never thought much of you. But what you've done for us has been amazing. I'm . . . I'm really impressed with you.'

Hatty looked at Georgia's face. Her worried expression had changed slightly. There was a look of determination there now. And Hatty knew she'd done her job. As she walked away from Georgia, towards the dressing rooms, she heard a cheer from the crowd. Then, above it all, Hawk's unmistakable chanting.

'*U-S-A! U-S-A! U-S-A!*'

The penalty had already been taken. Hatty looked

back at the goal. Adnan was picking the ball out of the net.

1–1.

Half an hour to go.

When Hatty was changed, she went to sit in the stand with the other fans. She looked at her watch. Five minutes to go. Still 1–1. The Squad needed two things.

First, a USA goal.

Second, for Adnan to suggest to the USA team that Hawk come to receive the cup with them. But Hatty knew that plans rarely work out exactly. So she wasn't surprised when the final whistle went and the match was still level. The game would end with a penalty shoot-out. Five shots each. Whichever team scored the most would win.

Rio decided who the five penalty takers were to be for England by going round and telling them who was doing it, then making sure they were happy to take one.

The five were him, Finn, Johnny, one of the other midfielders and Georgia. England would take the first penalty.

As Rio strode up to the take the first shot, Adnan stood close to Georgia. 'You OK?' he asked.

'Yeah.'

'You miss yours. I'll let all theirs in, OK.'

'Yeah.'

'Do you feel OK about that?'

'Yeah,' Georgia said.

Then she shifted her feet. 'No,' she said. 'No, I hate it. I just hope I don't have to be the one to miss, the one that loses us the game.'

Ten minutes later, Georgia placed the ball on the penalty spot. Every USA player and every England player had scored. If Georgia scored, the score would be 5–5 and the penalty shoot-out would go on. If she missed, England would lose. Her nightmare scenario had come true.

I can't do it, she said to herself. *I can't miss this.*

THE PENALTY

Hatty watched Georgia take three steps back, ready to strike the ball.

At the same time, she saw Adnan suggesting something to one of the USA players. The player – a boy – immediately glanced up at Hawk, then nodded to Adnan. Also, in the back of the stand, Hatty spotted two children – a boy and a girl – faces painted with the Stars and Stripes, waving another huge USA flag above them. Lily and Kester, in position, as planned. Everything was going to plan. All Hatty needed now was for Georgia to miss this penalty. But Hatty saw that there was something in Georgia's eyes that she didn't like.

She's not going to miss, Hatty thought. *She can't do it. I knew we should never have involved her. She's going to blow the whole thing.*

Hatty watched in horror as Georgia stepped forward and struck the ball hard. It flew towards the top corner of the net, easily beating the keeper. Hatty could only wince as it smacked on the underside of the crossbar, then bounced back *out* of the goal.

Georgia *had* missed.

The noise from the USA team and fans seemed to echo off the hills around them. Roaring. Whooping.

Then '*U-S-A . . . U-S-A . . . U-S-A . . .*'

Hatty stood still, pretending she was devastated, her eyes still on Georgia, who'd dropped to her knees and had all her teammates round her. Comforting her. Georgia had gone against all her instincts and missed the penalty on purpose. And now everyone was comforting her, even though she knew — and would always know — she'd missed it deliberately. And Hatty felt something like sympathy for Georgia.

But there was no time for feelings. Stage one was complete. The next stage was about to take place. The USA team were gesturing for Frank Hawk — the famous American businessman — to come out of the stands and join the celebrations.

Right on cue. Exactly to plan.

Hatty smiled at Lesh as Hawk stood, leaving the briefcase handcuffed to his assistant. Now — for a few minutes — Hawk was separated from his precious button.

It was working. Time for stage two.

Hatty looked to see the two face-painted children coming down from the back of the stand, waving their huge USA flag. Grinning. Whooping. Closing in on Hawk's assistant amid excited American celebrations. Hawk was on the pitch, shaking hands with all the children, posing for photographs. Grinning. Laughing. Distracted.

This couldn't be going better, Hatty thought as Lily and Kester moved in behind Hawk's assistant and jabbed the end of their flag into his leg. Immediately, the large American slumped into his seat, eased down by Kester, enough sedative in his bloodstream from the tip of the flag to keep him out cold for half an hour and out of action for a least another hour and a half.

And, because everyone was applauding, watching the trophy being presented, no one noticed a boy with his face painted like the Stars and Stripes removing the handcuff from the sidekick's wrist, then walking away with the briefcase, closely followed by the girl.

They had it. The button.

Hatty grinned at Lesh. But Lesh was not grinning back. There was something in his eyes. He was looking beyond Hatty. Hatty turned quickly.

At first, nothing seemed to be different. The American team was tossing the trophy around, surrounded by excited adults. And still the chanting.

'*U-S-A . . . U-S-A . . . U-S-A . . .*'

Then Hatty understood why Lesh looked alarmed. Hawk was no longer with them. He was on the far side of the stadium, jogging with a rucksack towards the gap at the far end of the pitch. Towards the hill the Squad had run up three days earlier.

Hatty hit the button on her watch, to make all the Squad stop and look at her.

She saw Lily and Kester stop their escape with the briefcase. She saw Adnan at the far side of the pitch, still in his keeper's kit and – again – Lesh's eyes on her.

She gestured towards Hawk just as he stopped to turn on the edge of the pitch. Hawk lifted his rucksack and pointed at it. He was wearing a broad grin.

Then he turned and disappeared into the woods.

Hatty lifted her watch to her mouth and pressed the speak button. 'He's still got his nuclear trigger. He's tricked us. We've blown it.'

THE BOMB

'Go after him!' Lesh shouted, taking out his pair of high-power binoculars. 'I'll monitor him from here. Everybody stay in radio contact.'

So, as the stadium emptied, and the Americans continued to congratulate themselves, the four children raced across the AstroTurf of the pitch, then into knee-deep snow outside, on the trail of Frank Hawk.

The American's footprints were clear. Only one track had been made in the half-metre of snow that blanketed the lower slopes of the hill. It led between two clusters of trees.

The Squad ran in single file, using the trail to speed their progress. A wind was whipping the surface of the snow into their eyes, obscuring their vision.

'When we hit the trees,' Kester ordered, 'spread out.'

They carried on their pursuit. Lily first, then Adnan, then Kester, then Hatty, watched – four hundred metres away at the stadium – by Lesh, who had been waiting for Hawk to emerge above the first clusters of trees, using his binoculars.

'No sign of Hawk above the trees,' Lesh reported on the radio, anxious suddenly.

'Roger,' Kester retorted.

Now that they'd reached the trees, they fanned out, one track becoming four as they started to climb the steeper hill.

'Take care,' Kester said in a low voice. 'He's possibly hiding. And he's probably armed.'

They moved on, through a deepening wood, the snow up to their hips now, the cold wind in their faces, scanning the hillside, desperate to find the American.

They all saw him at once and stopped, speechless.

He was standing on a rock that jutted out above the trees. He was holding a gun in one hand and a small device, about the same size as a SpyPhone.

'Well, if it isn't my friends from the mountain.' Hawk looked genuinely surprised.

'Hello again,' Kester said, trying to sound confident.

'And there was I thinking I'd filled you with enough lead to sink you to the bottom of that fjord.'

'We're tenacious,' Kester replied, seeing a smile pass across his enemy's face. But the smile was not about the mountainside hunting. It was about something else.

'It's empty,' Hawk shouted.

'What's empty?' Kester shouted back, trying to remain calm.

Hawk was armed and none of the children were: if he could get the American talking, it might buy them time.

'The briefcase. In your hand.' Frank Hawk was smiling.

Kester shook his head. The briefcase. It *was* still in his hand.

He tossed it to the side. It thwocked as it landed and sank slightly into the snow.

'This is perhaps what you're looking for?' Hawk held up the small device.

'What's that?' Kester asked, glad that the other three were remaining silent. The protocol for this kind of interaction was for one person to talk. They had to stick to that.

'It's the button. All I need to do is key in my memorized code and I detonate a nuclear device that will blow Tromsø and all its important politicians – and you – to your deaths.'

'And you,' Kester said. 'It'll kill you too.'

'No. Not me,' Frank Hawk said. 'Once I've tapped the code in, I have an hour to get to the other side of the mountain, away from the blast. It's not that big a bomb.'

'What about the fallout?' Kester asked. 'The device you're setting off is nuclear. It'll cast fallout for hundreds of kilometres. It'll be radioactive for decades. The first hours will kill everything within a hundred kilometres. Including you.'

He knew Hawk would have an answer for this. The American was hardly going to let off a nuclear bomb without having an exit strategy. Kester was asking so as to gather as much information as he could. Just in case there was a way out of this.

'You've done your homework,' Hawk smiled, glancing at his device and tapping its surface several times. 'But I've got a radioactive suit and respirator in here. And a boat, a day's walk away. Here . . .'

He tossed the device to Kester. And, for a second as it sailed through the air, Kester thought the American was surrendering. Adnan caught the device and handed it to his leader.

'What is it?' Kester asked Adnan.

'It says "armed",' Adnan replied.

'That's because it is armed.' Hawk laughed. 'What do you think I was doing just then? Phoning a friend? It'll go off in an hour. Unless . . .'

'Unless what?' Kester asked.

'Unless you know the series of eighteen numbers that is the code to deactivate it – the same one I just used to activate it. Oh . . . and you can only key one set of numbers in. If you get it wrong, there are no second chances.'

The four children looked at each other. Then, hearing a click, they all hit the floor, knowing Hawk was about to fire. Hawk was pointing his gun at the tree behind them. The clatter of bullets blasted over their heads, snapping branches off the trees and dumping woodchips and snow on the Squad.

Then Hawk was gone, running at a medium pace up the hill.

'Now what?' Hatty asked. And Kester realized the other three were looking at him, expecting an answer.

BASEBALL

Kester held his breath for a few seconds. Thinking. He didn't need long. It was clear what he had to do. He had two people in his team to deploy immediately to give them any chance of stopping a catastrophe.

He could see that Lily was already stretching her legs, strong lunges to warm her muscles, anticipating his orders before they came.

'Lily,' Kester said. 'You're the only one who can catch Hawk. Go after him. Stop him.'

'OK,' Lily replied, then she began to run up the hill. There was nothing else to say. Kester was right. Only she could keep up with the American. The others had to focus on deactivating the nuclear device.

'Come on. We need to talk to Lesh,' Kester said, turning to lead the other two in a run back towards the stadium.

Lily ran at a steady pace up the mountain. She saw a trail of footsteps heading along where she knew a track led up the side of the mountain, bordered by huge swathes of trees on either side. Hawk had chosen the most direct route up the mountain and Lily knew it would be foolish to go straight along the path after him. He would be expecting that. But Lily was a strong runner. She'd catch him soon enough if she took an alternative route. Yes, he was fit, but he was a muscular man, too heavy to be really fast on the mountains, like she was. So Lily went into the trees.

Kester, Adnan and Hatty stumbled through the snow, back in the footprints they'd made chasing after Hawk.

'How long does it say on the clock?' Kester asked.

Hatty glanced at it. 'Fifty-five minutes.'

'Lesh?' Kester was speaking into the microphone in his watch.

'Yes?'

'Hawk has activated the bomb. We've got less than an hour. We need to work out the code.'

'Any clues?'

'Nothing,' Kester said, slightly breathless as they ran.

'How many digits?'

'Eighteen.'

'I'll work it out,' Lesh said. 'Get here quickly.'

And soon they were all together, huddled round Lesh's SpyPad, desperate to crack the code.

'Think numbers,' Kester said. 'What numbers would you use to create a code? Something you could remember.'

'Birthdays?' Hatty suggested.

'His grandchildren's birthdays,' Adnan added.

Lesh immediately started to tap on the screen of his SpyPad. After two minutes of searching, he shook his head.

'I can find their names, where they live, but no dates of birth. We'll have to give up on that one.'

'Anyway, we need eighteen numbers. That wouldn't fit two kids' birthdays.'

'What else?' Kester asked. 'And we have to get this right. Whatever we key in we have to be convinced it's right. We only get one go.'

Ten minutes later, Lily had made good progress through the trees. Although the mountain was steeper here and the trees and their roots slowed her down, there was no snow on the ground and she was quickly level with Frank Hawk. She could see him through the trees, running a hundred paces, then squatting to study the track behind him. He had no idea he was being watched.

Her plan was to get ahead of him – way ahead of him – so that when he emerged at the treeline, where there was little vegetation and mostly rocks and stones, she would be ready and waiting.

But now she had to speed up, push herself further than she'd ever pushed herself before. And she had to work out how she was going to stop a man two times her body weight who was carrying at least two firearms.

'I know what it is.'

'What, Lesh?' Kester asked.

'Baseball,' Lesh explained.

'Baseball?' Hatty snapped. 'Why are you going on about baseball?'

'We know Hawk is sports mad. We know his favourite sport is baseball. And I've found out baseball fans remember statistics, like the top scores or when their team has won.'

'So?'

'Well, Hawk likes the Oakland Athletics.'

'Who?' Hatty asked.

'The Oakland Athletics. A baseball team from where he was brought up as a kid. He gives them money. All sorts.'

'And how does that fit in with the code, Lesh?' Hatty said impatiently.

'I've looked the Oakland Athletics up on the Internet. They've won the World Series nine times. All in the 1900s.'

'So?'

'Well, if you enter the years . . .'

'The years they won?'

'Yes. So if you enter all nine years – missing out the "nineteen" prefix – you've got eighteen numbers.'

Again there was a silence as the children faced each other.

'We're running out of time,' Hatty said. 'We have to choose something.'

A further silence.

'And this is as good as anything we've come up with,' Kester added.

'So, are we decided?' Lesh asked, looking at everyone's faces.

They looked into each other's eyes. But still none of them spoke. Then, together, they gave hesitant smiles.

'Yes,' they all said as one.

'So I do it?'

'You do it,' Kester agreed.

Lesh began to key in the eighteen numbers.

10–11–13–29–30–72–73–7 . . .

When Lily broke out of the trees, she was exhausted. She had never run so hard. But she had saved just enough energy to do what she had to do next.

She found two huge rocks, big enough to hide behind. They lay directly at the point in the path where Frank Hawk would emerge from the trees.

Lily began to pile up dozens of handgrenade-sized stones. Ready for Hawk. Her plan was simple. The moment he was in range, she would throw the rocks at him. Hard and fast. And if she hit him quickly – and hard enough – then she'd stop him drawing his gun. If she didn't, she'd be dead.

And soon he emerged, but not running. He was walking, breathless now. Lily had been right. He was too big to run up hills effectively. Lily waited with a rock in her right hand.

Hawk came closer.

Closer still.

She had to choose the right moment.

Then he slumped, hands on his knees, his bag at his side. He was shattered.

This was it.

Lily stood, the sun behind her, meaning he'd be blinded by the light coming off the snow.

The first stone hit him on the shoulder. Hawk twisted and fell back against the snow, but already he was reaching for the gun he had strapped across his chest. Two hands on it. Rolling into position. Lily had to finish this. Now.

So she stood between the large rocks and began to throw rock after rock, hard, down on to Hawk, not looking to see what he was doing now, just aware of where he was, making sure she hit him.

It could go one of two ways.

She could be hit by a bullet.
Or she could knock him out.

Lesh slowed as he keyed in the sixteenth, then seventeenth numbers: 4 and 8.

One left.

Once he hit the number 9, he would either have disarmed or set off a nuclear device. But he knew not to hesitate. There was no time.

He hit the button. The screen flickered and a single word came up on it.

DISARMED

Lesh smiled. Then he felt Kester's hand on his knee, Hatty's hand on his shoulder, saw Adnan beaming at him.

'You did it,' Kester said.

Lily's next three rocks hit Frank Hawk on his body. The fourth on his head. He was out cold. She'd done it.

Lily sprinted up to Hawk's unconscious body, wanting to tie him up somehow before he came round. When she reached him, she saw that his finger was on the trigger of his gun. He had come that close to shooting her.

First, Lily upturned Hawk's bag and found rope and some strong silver tape – the things he was taking to survive in the hills. They'd be very useful. She swiftly bound him with the tape, then looped the rope round his shoulders. She'd been trained in this: once you've put someone out of action, you had to make them immobile as quickly as you could.

Then she radioed down to the others.

TROMSØ TREATY

There were seven people in the Polar Suite that evening. One of them – the Prime Minister – was addressing the other six.

The Squad. Plus Julia.

The room looked even posher than it had before. There was a large round table in the centre of the room with a perfect white tablecloth. And on it, a feast.

'The conference has ended and –' the Prime Minister gazed momentarily out of his window at the Arctic beauty before him – 'I think we have high hopes that there's going to be an agreement. A Tromsø Treaty.'

'Between everyone?' Lesh asked, genuinely surprised.

'Yes,' the Prime Minister said. 'It seems that everyone knows that getting oil from under the ice – even after the ice has gone – will be hard. So they've decided to share their expertise and work it out together. Rather than have a war about it.'

'What about Canada, sir?' Lily asked.

'Canada is a good example,' the Prime Minister replied. 'They are less keen on getting at the oil and gas than on making sure the environment doesn't get damaged. That will be their area of expertise. They'll be part of all agreements within the treaty. They will make sure that damage to the environment is limited.'

Lily wondered if that would have been enough for Katiyana and White Fear. She suspected not.

The Prime Minister went on. 'Children, I have to thank you. I wish the world could thank you. But the world can never know what you've done. And, of course, they never will.'

'Thank you, sir,' Kester said on behalf of the Squad.

'Between you, you've saved the world. At least this part of the world. I want you to know how grateful I am. And – I'll be honest – I'm surprised. When I saw you, I thought . . . well . . . I had no idea children could be so . . . so effective.'

'Thank you, Prime Minister,' the five children said.

'Thank you, sir,' Julia echoed, staring at Hatty. 'Sir, we'd like you to meet another person who has helped with this mission.'

Hatty frowned, then walked to the door and opened it.

The Prime Minister was surprised to see another

girl, the same age as the Squad. She had blonde hair and looked very nervous.

'Good evening,' the Prime Minister said. 'And who are you, young lady?'

Georgia opened her mouth, but nothing came out. She was speechless with nerves. Hatty realized quickly that the other girl needed help. She decided to give it.

'This, Prime Minister, is another member of our football team.' Hatty was careful not to reveal Georgia's name. 'She became involved in our mission and – well, without her help – we would not have made a success of it. We wanted her to meet you and receive the credit she deserves.'

The Prime Minister put his hand out to shake it with Georgia.

'Thank you,' he said gravely. 'Thank you all.'

ALL AT SEA

A small fishing boat travelled up a fjord, in the high north of Norway. It was night. It was dark. But even though it was winter and snow covered everything, the sky was clear. Clear and black. A billion stars.

The Squad – plus Julia – were heading to the place where Katiyana's dead body had been dumped into the sea. They were sitting in a semicircle gazing at the beauty around them.

'OK,' Julia started, 'Let's talk.'

'Can I speak first?' Adnan broke in.

'Go on,' Kester said on behalf of the Squad.

'I've something to tell you.'

Lily, Lesh, Kester nor Hatty said a word. They knew what this was about. Adnan had made his decision.

'This is hard,' Adnan said and immediately, the other four knew what he had decided.

'You're leaving?' Julia asked in an unusually gentle voice. Adnan nodded.

And those were all the words that were needed.

The four embraced at the foot of that massive mountain in the Arctic Circle.

Later, after the group hug, the pats on the back, the laughing and the bit of crying, Lily found herself alone at the front of the boat, the bow slicing through the calm waters of Norway.

She was watching the mountains too, trying to work out the place where she thought Katiyana had been dumped into the sea. They were nearly there.

As she stared into the night, she wondered what it would be like if some uncle turned up for her. Would she leave the Squad? Could she give up the thrill of adventure, the satisfaction of stopping bad people doing bad things?

No, she decided. The only reason she'd leave this was if her mum and dad reappeared, like a miracle. But she knew that wasn't going to happen. The dead don't come back.

Then she decided it was time. 'It was about here,' she said. The others joined her at the bow of the boat.

Lesh wheeled himself to the edge. Kester and Lily lifted a small wreath of flowers and held it at the side of the boat. Adnan and Hatty joined them.

Then – with their hands holding the wreath together – they dropped it into the water.

'For Katiyana,' Lily said.

They stood in silence for several minutes with just the sound of the water lapping against the boat.

And then it happened. Something they'd not even thought about. A sort of miracle in itself.

The clouds above them began to move, shifting about. And they saw the most vivid shade of translucent green above them. An amazing display of colour against a backcloth of white mountains and pitch-black sea.

'The Northern Lights,' Kester said, smiling.

THANK YOUS

As always I need to say a huge thank you to my wife, Rebecca, who is my first reader, giving me blunt and brilliant feedback. She also does a thousand other things that help me make a living as a writer and I couldn't work – or live – without her.

Thank you also to my daughter, for telling me what she thinks of my books as I write them. I couldn't live without her either.

Thanks too to the writing group I have been part of, including James Nash, Anna Turner and Rachel Connor.

The Hurtigruten is a real shipping service that runs up and down the Norwegian coast. The crew of the *Nordlys* (meaning 'northern lights') were very helpful, especially Marie-Ann, who features as a character in the book. I was very sad to hear about the tragic accident on the *Nordlys*, just days after I had my tour of the ship and its engine room. I can thoroughly recommend a trip on the Hurtigruten. You can find out more about it at *www.hurtigruten.co.uk*

I also owe thanks to Norway and the several people who helped me in that country. It is a spectacularly beautiful place and its people are very nice. Special thanks go to Edvard Munch, Knut Hamsun, Eirik Bakke, Alf-Inge Haaland, Gunnar Halle and Frank Strandli.

Thank you to Rifleman Jim Sells, to whom this book is dedicated. Jim is great supporter of my career – and a friend. Thanks too to Diane Baker and David Luxton, who are also both very helpful and friends.

Thanks to my readers – Kael Baker and Mark Oldham – for their advice.

Finally, thank you to Puffin for publishing me and doing all they do. Especially Lindsey Hobbs, my lovely editor.

Ten things you (possibly) didn't know about TOM PALMER

Tom was possibly left as newborn in a box at the door of an adoption home in 1967.

He has got an adopted dad and a step-dad, but has never met his real dad.

Tom's best job – before being an author – was a milkman. He delivered milk for nine years.

He once scored two goals direct from the corner flag in the same game. It was very windy.

Tom did not read a book by himself until he was seventeen.

In 1990 Tom wrecked his knee while playing for Bulmershe College in Reading. He didn't warm up and has regretted it ever since.

He was the UK's 1997 Bookseller of the Year.

He met his wife in the Sahara Desert.

Tom has been to watch over 500 Leeds United games, with Leeds winning 307. He once went for twenty-one years without missing a home game. His wife has been ten times, with Leeds winning every time.

Tom once met George Best in a London pub. Tom wanted to borrow his newspaper to find out the football scores. George kindly obliged.

It all started with a Scarecrow.

Puffin is seventy years old.
Sounds ancient, doesn't it? But Puffin has never been so lively. We're always on the lookout for the next big idea, which is how it began all those years ago.

Penguin Books was a big idea from the mind of a man called Allen Lane, who in 1935 invented the quality paperback and changed the world. **And from great Penguins, great Puffins grew, changing the face of children's books forever.**

The first four Puffin Picture Books were hatched in 1940 and the first Puffin story book featured a man with broomstick arms called Worzel Gummidge. In 1967 Kaye Webb, Puffin Editor, started the Puffin Club, promising to **'make children into readers'**. She kept that promise and over 200,000 children became devoted Puffineers through their quarterly instalments of *Puffin Post*, which is now back for a new generation.

Many years from now, we hope you'll look back and remember Puffin with a smile. **No matter what your age or what you're into, there's a Puffin for everyone.** The possibilities are endless, but one thing is for sure: whether it's a picture book or a paperback, a sticker book or a hardback, **if it's got that little Puffin on it – it's bound to be good.**